THE SCREAMING FOREST

DARK RELICS SERIES

BOOK 1

RON RIPLEY

EDITED BY ANNE LAO
AND DAWN KLEMISH

ISBN: 979-8-89476-295-1
Copyright © 2025 by ScareStreet.com

Enter the Realm of Terror...

We'd like to take a moment to thank you for your support and invite you to join our VIP newsletter.

Dive deeper into the darkness with exclusive offers, early access to new releases, and bone-chilling deals when you sign up at www.ScareStreet.com.

Let the nightmares begin…

See you in the shadows,
Scare Street

PROLOGUE

It was starting to rain, it would soon be dark, and Jay's feet hurt. The woods crowded close on either side of the road. There hadn't been a car along in at least half an hour. The last one had sped by, ignoring her eager smile and her cardboard sign. Hitchhiking was a pain, but Jay hadn't been able to afford the bus fare.

She checked her phone again and got a flicker of one bar that faded. She was out in the boondocks, as her grandpa would call it. She wanted to check the Sanctuary site, just to make sure she was in the right area. The directions on the site had seemed very clear when she'd set out two days ago. Now, the names of towns and highways and turnoffs were all jumbled in her head.

She wished she'd written it all down and not relied on her phone to keep working.

A flicker of movement caught her eye, way off to the left. But as soon as she looked directly into the greenery, there was nothing but leaves and branches. Nothing but trees enduring a persistent drizzle that would, given time, soak her to the skin. It was probably a deer. Some cute little Bambi startled by her, big scary Jay.

She tried not to think about bears. Jay had no idea if this part of New England had any bears, and now was far too late to start worrying. Positive thinking would see her through. She was on the home stretch, not far from her destination.

Believe in something strongly enough, and it will become true. That was how the universe worked, she was almost sure.

Jay put her phone back in the pocket of her jeans, adjusted her backpack, and thought positively. *Sanctuary. Focus on that,* she told herself as she set off more briskly than before despite her aching feet. Positive thinking didn't seem to help with that. But Jay told herself it was probably a lack of faith, a failure of mental discipline. When she got to Sanctuary, they would help her become a stronger, better person.

Another movement, or was she imagining it? It was on the same side of the road, to Jay's left. And it seemed to be accompanied by the sound of a voice. Was it laughter? Or could it be sobbing? Were there any birds in these woods that sounded like a laughing or maybe sobbing person? Wildlife knowledge was not her strong suit. She'd found science cold and remote in high school, all about classification and detail. She preferred poetry and music.

Focus, she told herself, resolutely not looking to either side. *Focus on the goal.*

Jay cast her mind back to when she'd first come across the Sanctuary website while looking for spiritual truths online. Everything she'd read had seemed tailor-made for her. All the stuff about toxic families, false friends, and the shallowness of modern society. And when she had first started messaging with the Sanctuary people, they had been so interested, so kind, so intuitive about all her problems.

"Jay… you bad, bad girl…"

The voice called from somewhere on the left, where the woods seemed at their densest. This time, she had to stop and look around. No way had that been a bird. Somebody nearby was messing with her. Somebody who knew her name. Could it be one of the people from Sanctuary, one of her wise new friends?

"Hello?" she called, dismayed to hear how feeble her voice sounded. "Anybody there?"

A piercing scream was the only response, then sobbing. Fake sobbing, of course. Somebody was nearby, hiding from her, watching. Messing with her head. Like the bullies at school, only out here, it was worse. Anything might happen with no adults to see and intervene if things went too far. She began to run, despite her suffering feet and the weight of her backpack and damp clothes. She pounded along the winding road while the woodland to the left seemed to fill with laughter, interspersed with moans, shrieks, and cries. The sounds of pain and rage filled the air. There was an edge of craziness to it all.

There must have been more than one person, Jay realized, maybe six or seven. It was hard to tell because they never spoke except to tell her she was a bad girl. Sometimes, the accusation was yelled in fury; sometimes the tone seemed friendlier, more coaxing, which was worse.

"Come over here, bad girl. Come and have some fun."

The laughter that followed these taunts often turned to a mad shriek that gave her the shivers. Blood pounded in her ears, and the breath began to rasp in her throat. She was panicking now. Traces of movement became more substantial. She saw a slender figure slipping out of sight behind a massive tree trunk. A pair of eyes, piercing and dark, gazed at her from a clump of bushes, then vanished.

Despite all the taunting, nobody emerged from the woods.

After maybe a minute of running, Jay slowed, her initial panic fading, and checked again. Nobody within sight. A rational explanation occurred to her. Just local kids messing around. That would explain the hiding, laughing, and putting on silly voices.

"Okay," she gasped. "You've had your fun, you little creeps."

She resumed her plodding progress along the road, trying to refocus her mind on her destination. The voices faded but did not quite die out. There were screams in the distance that, now that she was calmer, sounded overdone, Halloween-horror-movie stuff. She even laughed at the hidden watchers, but the sound she made seemed forced.

Then she saw the stone. It was a slightly lopsided lump of granite on the roadside. As she got closer, she saw that it had been engraved with lettering many years earlier. The words were almost worn away, but she could still make out "1 MILE" below what must be the name of a town.

A mile. That's not so far.

She caught sight of the creepy guy a moment later.

He was standing about ten yards away, inside the woods, but not attempting to conceal himself. He was certainly not a kid—he might have been anywhere from thirty to fifty; it was hard to tell. The guy looked like he'd walked out of one of the reruns of Columbo her grandparents loved to watch. He had a mop of thick, curly hair, a chunky mustache, and was wearing an oversized leather jacket over a purple shirt open to show a medallion of some kind nestled in abundant chest hair. The stranger took a couple of paces toward her, and she saw he was wearing flared jeans and cowboy boots with three-inch heels.

"Run," he said. *"Run back the way you came, Jay. I can't protect you from them. Don't trust them, they lied to you. Liars, all liars. And murderers. Monsters! Nobody will help you, the whole town is in thrall to The Five."*

Jay was already backing away. Mustache Guy talked and dressed like a crazy person. She was prepared to run back the way she'd come, but she was so tired that the creep might well catch her, even in those boots. Then she remembered the pepper spray in her backpack. She swung the bag off her shoulders and to the ground, knelt, and started rummaging.

"No," the weirdo said, sounding alarmed more than threatening. *"No, that's useless, just go, Jay. I can't do any more…"*

Then, it happened. The weird guy shimmered and faded, his voice dying away. Jay stared, forgetting her search for the spray. At first, she was too surprised to feel anything but puzzlement. Then fear returned. And with it came the voices, closer now. This time, she could see more than glimpses of the screeching, laughing presences. First one, and then another. They appeared in the shadows, forms in dark-green shade cast by the trees. They were distorted, grotesque, barely human in shape. She screamed, and they screamed back at her as they advanced.

Ghosts. They're ghosts.

She ran, choosing a direction at random, heading past the milestone toward the town. Behind her, the shrieking, gibbering throng closed in. Jay wanted this to be a nightmare, to wake up in her bed and hear her mom calling her down for breakfast to get ready for school. Suddenly, all the burdens of that mundane life didn't seem so terrible.

Headlights appeared. It was a miracle. An SUV crested the low rise ahead of her. She began to wave her arms frantically, filled with dread at the thought it might swerve and leave her in the terror of the woods. But then the car slowed down and pulled over to the side of the road. Jay staggered up to it and leaned on the hood.

Inside the car was a middle-aged couple. The man driving was round-faced with a double chin. The woman was thinner and more severe-looking until she smiled at Jay. The strangers got out.

"Are you okay, Miss?" the woman asked.

"No, I'm scared!" Jay shouted and walked around the car.

Before she knew what she was doing, she'd grabbed the woman, burying her face in the front of her tweed overcoat. The woman patted Jay on the back.

"There, there," she said reassuringly. "Nothing to be scared of now."

"But there are ghosts in the trees," Jay sobbed. "I saw them and I heard them."

She felt the woman stiffen slightly. Then she gently let go of Jay and held her at arm's length.

"You saw ghosts? You're sure of that?"

"Yes," Jay said. "They were in the trees…"

She hesitated. Something about the woman seemed off. A normal person would surely question Jay's story, maybe even laugh. But the thin woman seemed curious, slightly puzzled.

"You believe me, right?" Jay asked.

"I do," said the woman. "It's interesting. We've never had a ghost seer before."

Jay stepped back, but the woman gripped her tightly. A strong arm wrapped around Jay from behind as she struggled. Something damp was pressed onto her face, covering her nose and mouth. The sweet chemical odor was overwhelming. She screamed but was already passing out. The darkening sky and the looming trees merged into a great ocean of blackness.

＊ ＊ ＊

Jay wasn't sure how long she had been unconscious. But she was somewhere else now, in an unfamiliar place. A yellow light flickered over wooden boards. She was bound, trussed up tightly so that her arms and legs could not move. There was a gag in her mouth, the cloth harsh against her flesh and unpleasantly damp with saliva. She could turn her head, though. She was on the floor of a shack. A table nearby bore the lamp that cast the erratic light. There were chairs, a door, and two boarded-up windows.

"She is awake. We can begin."

It was the voice of the woman from the SUV. Jay twisted around, writhing on the floor. Someone moved into her line of sight, then another, then three more. Jay stared in terror and confusion as the five looked down at her. They all wore hooded robes made of some dark red material. Inside each hood was an inhuman face. They were masks, she realized, each one a stylized animal visage. A wolf, a lion, an owl, a bull, and a reptile of some kind, perhaps a snake.

"It's all right, Jay," a man's voice said. "It will all be over soon."

"No, please," she begged. "Please, don't hurt me."

"Nobody is going to hurt you," someone else said. The voice of an old man.

Four stooped to lift her while the owl opened the cabin door and led the party outside. Jay struggled and pleaded with them, but nobody spoke to her again. She was being held face-up so the rain splashed down through the forest canopy onto her face, half-blinding her. The cowled figures began to chant words Jay did not understand. The cries from the ghosts, which first mingled with the chant, started to dwindle until all she could hear was the chanting.

The group slowed after just a couple of minutes. It was so dark now that Jay could see virtually nothing. But then, a yellow radiance revealed a small clearing and a roughly rectangular slab of rock. She struggled again, but her frantic efforts barely slowed her captors. They laid her on the slab and pinioned her ankles and wrists somehow.

"Please don't—" she began, but froze.

The weird guy was back. He stood at the edge of the clearing just within the pool of light cast by a hurricane lamp placed on a tree stump. Jay had thought him strange—creepy, even—but now, she realized that his eyes were compassionate. He spoke, and even though she could not hear him over the chanting, she could make out what he was saying.

"I'm sorry."

The five voices grew louder, and a darkness far deeper than any earthly night embraced her. She felt a sickening sensation as if she were falling. Then she was looking down at her body laying spreadeagle on the slab, the masked ones surrounding it. A filament of glowing mist seemed to link Jay to her body. Before she could try to make sense of this, the strand of light was ripped in half.

The pain that engulfed her then was more than any living being could bear.

CHAPTER 1

TAKING CARE OF BUSINESS

Craig Ellison walked into Hannigan's and immediately felt that special sense of relief. Part of it was the familiarity, of course. When a guy has a favorite pub, he starts to see it as a second home. Sometimes that creates problems at the first home, but Craig was lucky that way. The people waiting for him back at his apartment were very understanding.

Another plus was that Hannigan's was a friendly place—but not too friendly. If you wanted to sit alone and brood over life's injustices, nobody would bother you. If you wanted a quiet conversation with one person, this was the ideal place. Never too crowded, never quite empty, seldom if ever rambunctious.

It was a little crowded this evening, but nothing special for a Wednesday. And what mattered most to Craig was the quality of the clientele.

One very specific quality.

Every single one of them was alive.

"Hi, Craig!"

Melody, the barmaid, smiled at him as she zig-zagged past with about a dozen empty glasses. Her hair was an interesting confection of multi-colored braids this week. It changed as often as the weather, but her sunny personality was a constant factor.

"Keeping busy," he observed.

"Better too busy than too quiet," she said. "Stark's in his office as per usual."

Craig made a comical grimace.

"Guess I better go report in, then."

As he wove his way through the good-natured crowd, he wondered how much Melody and the other bar staff knew about his activities. The fact that he worked for Peregrine Stark was probably enough. Stark was the archetypal middleman, the fixer who always knew someone who could get stuff done. Weird stuff, usually, which was why he paid Craig handsomely. Not big bucks, exactly, but far more than Craig could earn otherwise.

Stark's office was metaphorical. He was seated at the end of the bar, on his own and with his usual bottle of root beer. The guy never seemed to touch alcohol. A few yards away, Harry, the manager of Hannigan's, was talking to someone Craig didn't recognize. The stranger was not too tall, and not too skinny, with a kind of battle-scarred look. For a second, Craig wondered if the man was one of Harry's old war buddies. But then he decided the age gap was too great. Harry was at least seventy, judging by things he'd let slip about Vietnam. This new guy looked closer to Craig's age but a lot more frayed around the edges.

Craig passed the newcomer and pulled up a stool so he could sit just outside Stark's personal space. As always, when he met his intermittent employer, Craig wondered if the man ever dressed well. He'd never seen Stark looking tidy and prosperous. Instead, the middleman wore mismatched clothes that screamed "thrift store", or maybe even "yard sale". He'd asked Stark about this once, and the man had only said that he didn't like to stand out. Craig thought that being too shabby made the guy conspicuous, even in an easygoing place like Hannigan's, but he kept that to himself. Craig knew Stark had limits and was not keen to test them.

"Ah, my friend," Stark rumbled, swiveling around on his stool. "I was so pleased to get your text. I assume you have made progress in our little investigation?"

Another thing that Craig found off-putting about Stark was his way of talking like a character in an old movie. Craig preferred blunt speakers like Harry and his no-nonsense approach, or Melody's cheerful openness. But neither of them paid him good money to do unusual jobs. Tasks that only someone with Craig's talent—or curse—could perform.

"Yeah, I found out more than I bargained for," Craig said.

Without being asked, Melody appeared, put a light beer in front of Craig, gave him a wink, and withdrew from earshot. Craig took a swig of the beer and then began to explain. His latest job had taken him to a 7-Eleven parking lot that had once been the site of a fine house. The house had been demolished, but the original owner was still around.

"Thaddeus Flyte is one angry ghost," Craig explained. "Took me a while to get him to talk. Must have been a piece of work when he was alive."

Stark made an impatient gesture, a fussy wiggle of the fingers.

"Yes, yes, you are a splendid ghost whisperer—but what did you find out?"

Craig quelled the desire to spin out the story between mouthfuls of beer. He felt he had earned a bonus for this one and didn't want to annoy Stark.

"Well, the descendants of Mr. Flyte were right about his fortune. Turns out, the old guy stashed away a lot of money and buried it in the cellar, which was filled in with concrete when they demolished the house."

"How much?" Stark demanded. "There was some confusion."

"According to Mr. Flyte, one hundred and fourteen thousand dollars in gold—South African Krugerrands," Craig said, enjoying the effect the revelation had. "Worth a heck of a lot more now, after fifty-odd years."

"Indeed," Stark said, reaching into his shabby jacket and taking out a checkbook. "I assume you have the precise location?"

Craig took a crumpled piece of paper out of his pocket. On it, he had sketched a rough rectangle, the parking lot, the front of the store, and its entrance. There was a cross where the gold coins were buried, and alongside Craig had written, "maybe 30 feet deep."

"Hmm," Stark said, studying the crude map. "Tricky to persuade the right people to let anyone dig there. So inconvenient."

Stark's eyes grew distant, telling Craig he was pondering his next move.

"A cover story about a faulty gas line, perhaps? I'm sure we can figure out something." He opened his checkbook and then patted his pockets.

This was part of their routine. Craig produced a pen, Stark thanked him and started to make out a check. Then he paused.

"Hold on. You said you discovered more than you bargained for? What might that have been?"

Craig took another swig of beer before wiping his lips. He noticed in the mirror behind the bar that the guy who'd been talking to Harry was now sitting just a few feet away, nursing a beer. Seen from this angle, the stranger looked even more battle-scarred than before. Their eyes met for a moment and Craig looked away. There were some people your instincts told you not to stare at in bars.

"Oh, yeah," he said, slightly rattled. "It was what Mr. Flyte said—about his sudden death?"

"Heart failure, I believe," Stark murmured. "But I suspect the man himself took a different view?"

"Yeah, his heart failed all right, but only because he was murdered," Craig said. "His son and daughter-in-law smothered the old miser with a pillow. They're long dead now, I told him that, but he was kind of emphatic about their children not getting a penny of his. And they are your clients, right?"

Stark made an airy gesture of dismissal.

"Details. Mere details. If the old man makes trouble, we can always hire a competent person to deal with him, but thank you for the heads-up. I think an extra five hundred for that information would…"

Stark did not finish his sentence and instead signed the check, tore it off, and handed it to Craig. Craig slipped it into his pocket, feeling furtive, vaguely ashamed. Not that he was a criminal—no laws existed concerning the manipulation of ghosts—but his employer knew how to make him feel like one. Perhaps insisting on doing business only face to face in a bar room was a mind game by Stark, a way of keeping Craig a little off-balance.

"Now," Stark continued, "if you are game, I have another, slightly more demanding job—one that might prove highly lucrative. But it involves quite literally leaving your comfort zone. You would have to go a few miles upstate. A little town called Grendon Mill. Have you heard of it?"

Craig shook his head. He noticed that Stark had not put away his checkbook.

"I don't like going to strange places, Perry, you know that. It's taken me years to make a home here, to make friends—well, friends of a kind. And I'm not good with strangers. Living strangers, anyhow."

Stark shook his head in what might have been genuine disappointment.

"Craig, you're still a young man. You're what, thirty-five? Yet you're already a stick in the mud who never wants to broaden his horizons. Life is about change and growth. It is also, I must remind you, about making money to pay the bills. What I'm about to offer you is a relatively simple job that will pay all your bills for the next six months or so. And I can give you fifty percent in advance, right now."

Craig gulped. Stark knew his weakness, but then again, it was probably the most common weakness in the world.

"Okay, what is this relatively simple job?" Craig asked.

Stark smiled and glanced past Craig. There was a scraping sound, and Craig realized that the tough-looking stranger had gotten up from his bar stool. He glanced into the mirror in time to see the man leaving. As the doors swung shut behind the stranger, Stark resumed.

"I do detest earwigging. Don't you?"

Craig shrugged.

"I think that guy's a friend of Harry's, so he's probably heard a lot of weird stuff."

Stark spent a second or two looking out onto the street, but there was no sign of the stranger.

"Oh well, back to business. I want you to go to Grendon Mill tomorrow and recover a certain item—an amulet, supposedly of great magical significance."

Craig frowned, wondering why one of Stark's many other operatives couldn't do something that simple. The shabby man pre-empted him before he could speak.

"You will be joined by another person, an independent contractor who comes highly recommended. A very experienced operative. She will meet you in Grendon Mill, and you will work together."

Craig felt an odd mixture of relief and apprehension. It was good to know he wasn't expected to work alone, but he had no idea who he'd been teamed with. If he asked, he was almost certain Stark would give him an evasive answer. He tried a workaround.

"Why would it take two people to find one small item? What's so special about this amulet?"

Stark sighed.

"Isn't it obvious? It's haunted. We need someone who can see and communicate with ghosts. Persuade the phantom to reveal the amulet's location. Oh, and ask the ghost very nicely not to make a nuisance when you bring the amulet to me. Your honest, sincere approach is bound to prevail. And the fact that ghosts can't kill you is an undeniable boon. The other operative is just there to provide backup, moral support, and perhaps some occult expertise. Which, almost certainly, won't be needed."

Craig doubted if things would be that simple. Ghosts were not always open to persuasion, even though Craig had a knack for getting through to them. It was contact with the living that he struggled with.

"This other person you mentioned—do I get her name?"

Stark told him the woman's first name. Tara. Craig knew better than to demand any more. To Stark, arcane knowledge was power, and he tended to hoard facts in much the same way as old man Flyte had hoarded his gold. To Craig, it was just another source of anxiety.

"Until you meet her in Grendon Mill, all communication must be through me, though," he added. "She prefers to be incognito, at least at first. Or should that be incognita? For a lady? Latin never was my strong point."

Craig groaned inwardly. If they gave out medals for being pretentious, Stark would have amassed an impressive collection.

"Why the cloak-and-dagger stuff?" he asked bluntly. "It's me going out there, I need to know something. Like what does this amulet look like?"

The middleman admitted, with a hint of acerbity, that he didn't know what it looked like.

"Others are on the trail of this amulet, I believe," Stark went on. "It's the way of collectors—news gets out that a lost item might be located somewhere, and the information spreads like wildfire in their little world. And if anyone in Grendon Mill gets wind of it, they might claim ownership or try to steal the pesky thing. There are some very dishonest people in this world. So, be discreet, do your ghost-whisperer act, and swoop in first."

"You won't even give me a picture of this expert I'm supposed to meet?" Craig asked.

"I'm afraid not—security, you know. Just let me know when you arrive, and I will send the details. Same goes for her, of course. And now, if you will excuse me, I must pay a visit to the little boys' room and then toddle home."

Stark slid off the bar stool and stretched, his mismatched clothing falling into new patterns of rumpled cheapness.

"Do I get travel expenses, hotel, those kinds of things?" Craig asked.

"Of course," Stark said. "I'll fill out a blank check when I get back, and you can just put in the amount. I trust you not to try and gyp me."

Craig would never have dared, and Stark knew it. The limits of Stark's knowledge, malice, and abilities were very nebulous to Craig, and he preferred to keep it that way. He finished his beer, paid for it and chatted with Melody for a few minutes, and then took the second check when Stark returned. The streetlights were coming on now, revealing the thin drizzle spattering the pub window.

"Guess I'd better be going," Craig said. "And, uh, thanks, I guess."

"Sleep tight, have plenty of rest," Stark said cheerfully. "You've got a long journey ahead of you."

Outside, Craig turned up his jacket collar against the rain, which was coming on stronger now. He set off at a brisk pace, keen to get home before a full-on downpour began. But as he crossed the road, he noticed the man from earlier standing in the mouth of an alleyway. The stranger was deep in conversation with someone. As Craig got closer to the alley, he saw that the person the man was talking to was the ghost of a labor organizer from the 1890s. The man had been beaten to death by hired strikebreakers. That meant the stranger was a seer, too. But not, apparently, one known to Stark.

The man left the ghost and walked a few paces to intercept Craig, who gave up on the idea of ignoring him.

"Yeah?" Craig said, trying to sound tough and worldly.

"You're Craig Ellison, right? You get information from ghosts."

The other man's voice was deep and harsh, sounding as scarred as his face. And there was something else. Now that he had gotten a good look at the guy, Craig could see a world of suffering. He'd seen eyes like those before, but never in a living man's face. This was not a man to mess with.

"Yeah, some," Craig replied.

"Maybe you can help me. I'm looking for some kids who went missing 'round these parts. A few passed through here. At least one told a friend they were heading for Grendon Mill."

Craig grew tense. Was this one of the relic hunters Stark had mentioned? One with a good cover story? Yet the stranger seemed straightforward enough. He had taken out a phone and was working on the screen. Then he held it up so Craig could see a picture of a pretty girl in a Nirvana T-shirt. She was smiling and holding up her fingers in a peace sign. The stranger swiped the screen to reveal a bespectacled, serious-looking boy of around sixteen. Then another picture, this one of a chubby girl clutching a very large, grumpy-looking cat.

"Just a few of them. There's maybe a dozen, all vanished upstate over the past thirty years or more," the stranger went on. "Ring any bells?"

Craig had never seen any of the youngsters before and said so.

"Okay," the stranger said, putting away his phone. "But if you get any information, I'd appreciate it. Here. Email and phone number."

A gnarled hand with a missing finger held out a folded sheet of notepaper. Craig took it but didn't unfold it at once, his eye caught by the glint of metal on the stranger's fingers.

"Are those steel rings?"

"Iron," the scarred man said. "Iron has power over ghosts. You knew that, right?"

Craig hadn't known it, and his face must have given away his ignorance. The stranger frowned.

"Surprised you've gotten this far without needing to punch a few ghosts. You've led a charmed life. But luck runs out, you know? Iron gives you an edge. Get yourself some. Especially in your line of work..." the stranger's voice trailed off as he nodded toward the direction of the pub. Presumably referring to Stark.

Craig was so surprised by the idea that he couldn't think of anything to say. The other man stood for a moment, streetlights glistening on the rain running down his face, then gave a slight nod and walked off. Craig realized he was holding his breath.

He set off home, wondering if he should report the encounter to

Stark. That guy could have been one of the rivals searching for the amulet. A string-of-missing-persons story would be a good cover.

Then he thought about the stranger's eyes and the depths of pain he had seen there. The sort of pain he'd seen in the eyes of ghosts who had lived and died in torment. Craig decided to keep the brief encounter to himself for now.

After all, Stark didn't tell him everything, either.

CHAPTER 2

GROUP DISCUSSION

"Don't trust that asshole," Billy said. "Stark's a slippery sonofabitch."

Craig valued the dead biker's opinion, though he sometimes doubted Billy's judgment. Anyone who rammed their Harley-Davidson into a brick wall at more than a hundred miles per hour could be said to have a few character flaws. In this case, though, Billy's views meshed with Craig's.

The other ghosts in his tiny living room were more circumspect, but none of them seemed too keen on Craig leaving town. Leroy, the ghost of a janitor who had died sometime in the 1970s, disapproved of all shady activity. He had high-minded principles. Leroy had marched on Washington with Martin Luther King Jr. and mentioned the fact on every possible occasion.

Chloe, the emo girl, was less forthright. She simply looked troubled. She had become a fixture in their meetings since Craig had formed the support group. Sometimes, he thought she had a crush on him. But more often, he suspected she saw him as a well-meaning but naïve uncle. Or maybe a dimwitted older brother. Someone who needed looking after, anyhow.

"Guys," Craig said, waving the checks in the air, "money talks. And right now, it's telling me to get moving. I know Stark is shady, probably in more ways than we can imagine. But I can only afford this place because the guy pays me better than any legitimate employer. I have to have a place that's inside your overlapping radiuses of activity. Or maybe it's radii?"

"Radiuses is kind of clunky," Billy commented. "Best stick to the Latin usage, it's more authentic."

"That's fine in theory," Leroy said, "but ray-dee-eye? Sounds like a third-rate rap artist."

The ghosts were prone to spin off in tangents in conversation. Craig raised his voice.

"Doesn't really matter. The point stands. Remember that place I had to live in when I was a nightwatchman?"

Chloe shuddered. Billy swore. Leroy looked disapprovingly at Billy, then spoke.

"I get that. A man must provide for himself. Do what needs to be done. But this upstate gig, do you think it's safe?"

Craig sighed and decided to go over it again.

"As far as I know, I just need to persuade a ghost to reveal where this amulet is. They want me to sweet-talk the guy so I can deliver the item to Stark, who'll get paid by some collector who probably has more money than sense."

"But you don't even know the spook's name, or what he looks like," Billy grunted. "Or where in this one-horse town he hangs out."

Craig rolled his eyes heavenward.

"I can ask other ghosts, Billy," he pointed out. "You guys all know each other in this city. In a small town like Grendon Mill, it'll be child's play."

Leroy looked uncertain.

"My Aunt Bessie always said, 'Overconfidence is the enemy of achievement.'"

Craig sighed and stood. He was not going to debate the wisdom of Aunt Bessie, or any of Leroy's numerous relatives, some of whom Craig suspected were fictional. They might still be talking come midnight if he did not put his foot down.

"Guys, I'll be fine. Now, if you don't mind, I'd like to shower, brush my teeth, and go to bed. I've got to be up early tomorrow."

For mercy, the ghosts faded away without grumbling. The one

advantage of Craig's talent as a seer was that he could make sure he wasn't being watched, in the shower or elsewhere. Regular people couldn't, and that tickled him sometimes. Whenever a politician, tycoon, or celebrity was being a massive jerk—which happened most days—Craig wondered how many ghosts watched them when they were on the toilet or having sex. And what the ghosts had to say about it. Ghostly voyeurs, in Craig's experience, often passed pithy comments when they observed the living at their most undignified.

Sleep was long in coming that night. Craig kept going over the job. He had booked a train ticket and a hotel room. He had packed a bag. He had plenty of money. It was almost too good to be true. So, it probably was. Stark had landed him in hot water several times before. When Craig thought about the worst occasion, the little toe on his right foot began to tingle. Which was interesting because that particular toe wasn't there anymore.

"Go to sleep, ya doofus," he murmured.

He sat up, punched his pillow into submission, then lay down facing the bedroom door. A little light strayed through a gap in the curtains. Craig decided to close that gap. All he had to do was get out of bed, walk a few paces, reach up…

Then he found someone leaning over him. He yelped in dismay before the figure spoke.

"It's only me."

"Chloe?"

The ghosts usually treated his bedroom as off-limits, though Billy was not one for rules and sometimes barged in when he had to vent. Chloe had never intruded before.

"What is it?" he whispered.

"It's about Grendon Mill," she said. "I remembered something. I had a friend… in high school. I think she went there."

Craig sat up, heart pounding. It was a breakthrough of sorts for Chloe to reveal anything about her past. If a ghost could unburden themselves to him, reveal the full truth about their life and death, they could move on. This was not an ideal time, but Craig felt he had to give it the old college try.

"Okay," he said. "This friend, what was her name?"

"Nikki," said Chloe, and spelled it out. "She always insisted on the two Ks."

"Why did she go to Grendon Mill?"

The girl hesitated and Craig saw the shadowy form shimmer and fade a little, a sign of strong emotion. A powerful memory had disturbed Chloe.

"I'm not sure," the girl said after her outline had solidified somewhat. "I think it was a kind of rock festival—or maybe a secret rave, that kind of thing? They were fashionable back then. I know she had her hair dyed bright blue, like electric blue. It looked amazing. She wanted me to go too, but… I was going through some things. So, she went by herself. I tried to talk her out of it—you know, traveling alone to a place she'd never been before? But—"

"And she never came back?" Craig asked.

He could just make out Chloe shaking her head.

"I never found out for sure. She left the week before I died. But sometimes, when it's really quiet, I hear screams in the night. Screams coming from really far away. And I know it's Nikki—somehow, I just know."

The vague outline of the girl was gone a moment later. Craig was left alone in the dark and wondered just how much sleep he was going to lose thanks to that story. He lay awake for at least an hour but eventually sank into a dreamless slumber. He was woken by a stinging sensation as if someone had pierced his shoulder with a tiny, but very sharp, icicle. It took him a moment to grasp what had happened.

"Sorry," Leroy said, stepping back from the bed. "But I didn't know what else to do, my man. You slept through your alarm. You don't wanna miss your train."

Craig washed and dressed hastily and decided not to waste time making breakfast. He was rebuked for this by Leroy, whose grandma always said, "Breakfast was the only meal a man should never skip." Craig insisted he would get something on the train and left, almost forgetting his phone in the process.

His next-door neighbor peeked out of her front door as he scurried toward the stairwell. It was a small, elderly woman who never seemed to go out. She gave the kind of look he'd seen many times before. She had heard him talking to the ghosts and drawn an obvious conclusion. He smiled, wondering how she would react if she knew he did not, in fact, live alone.

As he descended the stairs two at a time, he thought about how ghosts watched people the way some people watched reality TV. And chuckled.

CHAPTER 3

STRANGERS ON A TRAIN

The railroad car was not crowded, and Craig had a couple of seats to himself. He put his bag in one and sat in the other, next to the window. The train pulled out of the station, and for the first time in years, Craig found himself leaving his adopted hometown. As the suburbs gave way to fields and then forested hills, he felt a tug of panic, urging him to go back. But he could hardly pull the emergency handle, or whatever they called it, and then tell the guard, "I was homesick, and I'm no good with people."

He smiled at his immaturity, wishing he could cure the problem as easily as he could identify it. Then, he took out a book and started to read. It was a cheap novel he had lying around for weeks at home, some kind of thriller by a bestselling author. The first few pages were just absorbing enough to dispel his anxiety. He followed the adventures of the big, tough, no-nonsense hero for a whole chapter. But just as the action shifted from New York to Paris, the paperback seemed to become very heavy, and he let it fall into his lap.

"Good book?"

The words snapped Craig out of an uneasy dream that left a vague impression of trees and faces between them. Someone was sitting opposite him—an old man, black, with very white hair cropped closely. He might have been about sixty, but it was hard to tell. The stranger wore the uniform of the railroad company. The jacket looked freshly pressed, and the buttons gleamed. Craig found himself returning the older man's open, warm smile.

"Oh, this?" He held up the novel. "I guess it's okay, but I was tired, so…"

The old man nodded.

"Traveling up and down this line, I see people reading all kinds of books. The titles and the authors change over the years, but the readers are kind of similar, you know?"

Craig nodded, though he wasn't sure he did know.

"Some people turn right to the end," the man went on. "I could never understand that, reading the last page to see whodunnit. Do you do that?"

Craig shook his head, smiling again.

"Seems kind of dumb—the whole point is the journey. Through the story, I mean. With the characters."

"Exactly," the railroad man said. "But some people want instant gratification. The way our world's going, that's gonna be the only kind available soon."

That caused a hiatus in the conversation. The stranger looked out of the window at the countryside that seemed to roll by like an old-fashioned panoramic view. They passed a tumbledown structure that might once have been a factory. Suddenly, Craig saw men on fire, running from the building. They passed through a field without troubling the tall grass. He imagined the ghosts' screams and was glad he could not hear them. He closed his eyes and turned away.

"Every day," the old man said. "Regular as clockwork. The way I figure it, that accident happened when a train was passing, and they're kind of stuck in that loop. You might think differently, of course."

Craig stared at the old man and then slumped back in his seat. Of course, the old guy was a ghost. The uniform was not the same as the Amtrak staff he'd encountered earlier. It was a little outdated.

The stranger talked on, going back to his original theme.

"Then there are people who keep going over the same pages—I've seen that a few times. Turning back a few pages, going over the same ground. And some people want to finish a book before the journey ends.

I see them speeding up, kind of skimming, as the train gets closer to the station. That's funny."

Another pause.

"Name's Sam, by the way. Samuel Jefferson Carter, but everyone just calls me Sam—or maybe Railroad Sam."

Craig smiled again and gave his name.

"Yeah, I know," Sam said. "You're kind of a celebrity 'round these parts. The guy who sees ghosts, talks to them, doesn't judge, tries to help. Word gets around. You're okay, son."

Craig felt himself reddening. He was not used to praise, even the mild kind. They stared out the window for a few more minutes.

"When did you die?" Craig asked finally.

Sam made a gravelly sound that might have been a chuckle.

"Kind of a personal question, son—like asking a lady her age. Or her weight."

"Sometimes," Craig said, "all it takes to pass on is—well, unburdening yourself. Telling the real story, your story, with no revisions or omissions."

Sam stood and raised his hands as if to ward off Craig's suggestion.

"Oh no, son, you got me wrong. I don't want to pass on, I just wanted to have a little chat. This was my life, the railroad. Why shouldn't it be my death? I'm not hurting anyone."

The old man stepped into the aisle and then hesitated.

"Where are you going, anyway? And that is a personal question too, I know. But will you humor a dead guy?"

"A town called Grendon Mill. I'll have to get the bus the last few miles 'cause it's kind of remote, but I guess it won't take too long…"

Craig paused. Sam's face had changed, no longer benign and untroubled.

"Is there a problem?"

The old man shrugged.

"Like I said, you hear things, riding the rails all the time. Something bad happened at Grendon Mill, way back when I was still on the payroll and had a pulse. Bunch of people died. Bad juju. Best avoided. You got family there, or friends?"

"No. I'm going to do a job, just for a day or two," Craig said, trying to sound reassuring, wanting to bolster his own confidence.

Sam spent a few moments looking down at him and then laughed.

"Here's me telling you spooky stories, quite the twist. Guess you'll be okay if you're not there for too long. Anyway, be seeing you on the way home. Have a safe journey."

And with that, Samuel Jefferson Carter walked off down the aisle as he had done so many times in life. Craig returned to his book, felt sleep start to reclaim him, and then turned to the last page. It seemed that the hero got together with the sexy scientist who initially had not liked or trusted him. Flipping back a couple of pages, it seemed the duo had saved the world from a complex conspiracy of some kind.

Craig laid the book in his lap and peered out at the passing world. He halfway expected Sam to turn up again, but the old guy had presumably found something more interesting elsewhere on the train. At the station nearest to Grendon Mill, Craig got off and walked a short distance to the bus station. The next bus was not scheduled to leave for half an hour. He was alone in an unfamiliar town.

This sort of thing is a minor inconvenience to a normal person, he thought. *They would get coffee. I should act like a normal person.*

He walked out of the bus station and went to a small café. The place was striving for quirkiness by calling itself *Cup and Cake*. It did indeed sell what purported to be homemade cupcakes. Craig didn't have a sweet tooth, but as he ordered, he decided to try one. He sat at a table by the window and waited for his name to be called as he watched the world go by. No ghosts were apparent at first. This was often the way in urban areas, where the sheer number of people alive today outweighed the handful of phantoms from earlier times.

After five minutes or so, a woman approached the window. She was dressed in a motley array of clothes, mismatched and shabby. Her boots were stuffed with what looked like crumpled newspaper. A homeless person, clad for chilly spring nights. Feeling awkward, Craig looked away, but he was aware of her getting closer to the glass.

"Clay? I got a mochaccino for Clay?"

Clay? How could they get my name wrong? Craig thought, getting up and waving at the barista. *No way my writing is that bad. It's like they take a special course or something. Misreading 101.*

He collected his coffee and returned to the table and his slightly overpriced cupcake. The homeless woman was still outside, face pressed against the glass. A security guard, paunchy and slow, walked along just a few yards behind her. He glanced into the shop and frowned at Craig, who looked down into his coffee cup.

The woman passed through the glass and sat at Craig's table.

"Long time since I had something nice," she said, gazing avidly at Craig's little cake. "Bet it tastes good. What flavor is it?"

Craig sighed. It would be impolite not to have a conversation. He might even help. He took a deep breath and prepared to become, not for the first time, the weird guy sitting alone, seemingly talking to himself.

But it would pass the time until he caught his bus.

CHAPTER 4

GRENDON MILL

Craig dozed off on the bus, waking intermittently to the blare of a horn or the hydraulic hiss of the door. He saw no ghosts at the various stops, or at least none that made themselves known to him. He wondered idly how many people died on public transportation vehicles. At first, he thought it must be hundreds a year in this state alone. He took out his phone and looked up some statistics but gave up after a few minutes. It was morbid.

He switched to Google Maps to find out where he was. Not far from Grendon Mill, it turned out. The winding road led through a forest. Craig zoomed in and out, looking for the name. But it seemed the woods were just that—an anonymous expanse of old-growth trees.

He moved to Wikipedia to look at the entry on Grendon Mill. It was short and dull. The town had been founded by a lumber baron in 1874. The mill flourished until the Great Depression. World War II had brought a brief revival, thanks to increased demand for timber. After the war, things were okay, but then the town saw a second, more severe decline in the lumber industry. The mill closed in the '60s, but tourism and antiquing provided some employment. It was a familiar story.

Craig searched further, looking for the "bad juju" Sam had mentioned. He eventually found something in a brief news report. It seemed that in October 1977, a fire broke out on the outskirts of town. The disused lumber mill burned down and several people died. It was unclear whether there had been four or five fatalities. An arsonist used gasoline to torch the building, and only partial remains were found. However, four local men were declared missing after the fire. The motive for the crime was unknown.

Well, Craig thought, *I might get some information from the dead at the site of that fire.*

His phone informed him that he had lost internet connection, and he took to gazing out the window. After passing through some farmland, they entered a dense forest. Craig felt a twinge of unease. Although it was almost midday, the darkness under the trees seemed to absorb all the light and color from the world. It was probably his imagination. He peered into the trees, hoping to see some sign of human activity, or maybe a deer. A bird, at least. But nothing seemed to stir.

He was relieved when the bus emerged from the forest, and they reached the outskirts of the town. Several minutes more, and he found himself exiting at a nondescript bus station by the town square.

Grendon Mill was small and bordered on picturesque. There were some old-style clapboard houses and a pleasant town square, complete with an ornamental fountain. Aside from some stores, there was a decent-sized, white-painted church, a compact town hall, and a library that doubled as a museum. Craig got the lay of the land as he walked around the square, stretching the numbness from his legs, and wondering where to start.

Where are the ghosts?

In most towns, the dead were self-evident by their outdated clothes or unusual behavior. It was common for a new ghost to resist staring into the faces of the oblivious living or goofing around in some way. However, that novelty wore off after a while. Then those of a bleaker disposition would often just stand on the street, lamenting their fate and wishing for oblivion. Either way, Craig had never had trouble finding them. But in Grendon Mill, it seemed he was faced with a challenge.

He walked around the town square again. The bus pulled out, and the passengers had mostly dispersed. The exception was a tall, dark-haired woman who had given Craig a direct stare as they disembarked. Now, she sat by the water fountain checking her phone. She glanced up at him, then returned her attention to the little screen and continued to make scrolling gestures. Stark had assured him that the mysterious Tara would contact him—he was not to approach her. The woman by the fountain looked smart and competent. She was also kind of hot, he decided, in an athletic kind of way.

Focus, he reminded himself. *You're waiting for a partner for a job, not a date.*

Craig ambled along a few more paces until the fountain obscured the woman's view of him. Two could play the cloak-and-dagger game. Then he remembered that he was supposed to report in. He sent Stark a terse text.

Arrived at GM safely. Where is T?

He spent thirty seconds wondering if there would be an immediate reply then decided to get something done instead. He checked the location of his hotel. It was about a quarter mile up the road. His bag was not too heavy; he could walk it.

He decided to get something to eat before checking in. A place called Dinah's Diner sat just off the square. He went over to check it out and found it tacky but acceptable. He was taken aback when he saw the prices, then realized they must be geared to the tourist trade. Locals probably ate elsewhere. At home, say.

Besides, he thought, *Stark is paying expenses.*

Buoyed by the thought of a free lunch, Craig ordered the diner's all-day big breakfast offering fried eggs, bacon, fried bread, and pancakes with syrup. As he tucked into the meal, he discreetly observed the people around him just in case a ghost moved among them. But the wait staff was chatting with each other and the clientele. The customers were equally lively.

Craig switched his attention to the street, again wondering where the ghosts of Grendon Mill might lurk. This was a town built on the lumber trade in the late 1800s. Therefore, logically, several people must have died from industrial injuries and disease, as well as other causes like the Spanish Flu pandemic. He studied the passersby but saw only living men, women, and children going about their daily lives.

Had everyone who died in Grendon Mill just moved on? Had everyone been so happy in life that they had no reason to linger on the earthly plane? No unfinished business? No unspent rage? No one they desperately wanted to watch over? What the hell was Craig supposed to do with no ghosts to question? He wasn't a detective.

Calm down, he told himself. *You've hardly begun to explore. For all you know, your hotel is haunted. Ghosts are more often found in buildings than on the streets. And this Tara person might have some leads. You're part of a team, remember that. You're not doing this alone.*

That cheered him up, and he finished his pancakes with gusto before ordering a slice of key lime pie for dessert. The waitress came by every few minutes to freshen his coffee. He had just called for the check when someone new came in—a paunchy guy of about fifty in a tan uniform. The waitress greeted the newcomer as "Chief".

The lawman paused in the doorway and cast an eye around the clientele. Craig was never quite sure how to respond to cops. Behaving naturally was the sensible option, but he tended to forget how. A life as an outsider had made him more squirrelly than most people. He feigned fascination with his half-eaten dessert. His attempt to go unremarkable failed miserably—the police chief ambled over and stopped by his table.

"Well, good day to you, sir."

It was a friendly opening. Craig, still nervous, looked up and returned the greeting.

"Just arrived?" the cop asked.

"Yes," he said, then felt he should add something. "It's a nice town."

"We like to think so. Nothing spectacular, of course, but pleasant. I'm

Chuck Halloran, by the way. Any problems, you just pop into the office and let me know. We want visitors to go home and tell everyone this is a friendly little place—because it is. Anyhow, I won't take up any more of your time. That pie sure looks good."

Craig introduced himself and thanked the chief. After a few more pleasantries, Halloran ambled over to the counter and parked his substantial posterior on a stool. The cop then started chatting with the staff, throwing out the odd remark to customers who were evidently locals.

Craig wondered if local law enforcement was aware of the amulet, or at least had noticed strangers asking questions. He decided to keep a low profile until Stark's other agent showed up.

After he'd paid for his meal and left a generous tip, Craig walked back to the town square. Some benches were arranged around the fountain, facing outward, and an old man sat on one of them. People walked by without sparing him a glance as if he was invisible. This was promising.

As Craig approached, the man looked up and squinted. He was a small man, with thinning, unruly gray hair, and a very wrinkled face. He reminded Craig of a gnome in a fairytale, or maybe Yoda. Something about the guy's clothes struck a chord. He remembered Sam, the railroad man. This stranger was wearing an old-fashioned military greatcoat several sizes too big. His small, wrinkled face was half obscured by the high collar. A row of faded medal ribbons sat over the left breast.

"Mind if I sit here?" Craig asked.

"'Tis a free country," croaked the old man, looking surprised. "Guess you're new in town? Never seen you before. I'm sure I'd remember."

Craig sat, setting his bag between himself and the stranger.

"Just got in this morning," he replied.

"That right? Well, well, well," the old man said. "And you thought you'd come sit and talk to me?"

"That's right," Craig said brightly. "Do you often sit here, watching the world go by?"

"I guess so," the stranger replied. "Not much else to do. You're the first person who's talked to me in a long time."

Craig felt a pang of sympathy. Was this poor guy the only ghost in town, or at least in this area?

"I like talking to… to people with interesting stories to tell. I'm into local history, folklore, stuff like that."

The old man perked up at this and twisted around to face Craig.

"Ah, well, if you like stories, I've got a few. I'm what you might call a 'permanent fixture' here. And I don't get much opportunity to talk."

This was very promising. Now that the man had turned toward the noonday sun, Craig could see that his pale blue eyes had a slightly unfocused, faraway look that he'd often seen in ghosts. They got so used to haunting the same limited area and seeing the same unresponsive mortals that they barely noticed their surroundings. It was the ghostly equivalent of the thousand-yard stare.

"So, you must have seen a lot of changes around here?" Craig prompted.

The old man launched into a rambling monologue about the lumber mill, various wars, layoffs, young people today, the state of the world, ridiculous prices, and the general lack of respect for the elderly. Craig smiled indulgently, waiting for some hint of what he was after. When the old guy trailed off, however, he had to search for another question.

"I heard something unusual happened here way back in the seventies. A fire or something?"

The old man looked surprised, then pensive. Finally, he brightened.

"Oh yeah, that was the old lumber mill—it burned down. There were some people inside, they said. Strange, because it'd been closed down for years. Now they take the wood down to—where is it?—somewhere downriver. Pelham? Davenport? I used to know…"

More rambling led Craig no nearer to his objective. He waited for a pause and then decided to stop beating around the bush.

"Look, I know this is strange," he said, "but the reason I'm asking you about the past is because I'm looking for something. A lost object. It's an amulet, and it's linked to a ghost."

"A ghost?" The old man narrowed his eyes.

"Yes, a ghost—you know how ghosts tend to stay tied to some significant object or location after they die?"

The old man laughed uncertainly.

"Now, you wouldn't be messin' with me, would you, son?"

"No," Craig said, "I'm surprised you didn't know—I mean, you are tied to this location, right? Like, the fountain, or the town hall, maybe? I noticed you looking up at the town hall…"

The old man's expression changed again. This time, it showed alarm mixed with anger. He scrambled to his feet and backed away from Craig.

"What the hell is wrong with you? I'm not dead! I'm just old, you crazy sumbitch."

With that, the old man turned and stomped off around the fountain, muttering things Craig was glad he couldn't hear.

"Damn," Craig said. "Thought I had one."

CHAPTER 5

A WOMAN ON A MISSION

After his failure at the fountain, Craig traipsed up the main road to the hotel where he had booked a room. At reception, he again tried out his story about being a history enthusiast. He almost claimed to have a blog but stopped himself just in time. Most people had better things to do than check strangers' blogs, but it would be just his luck to encounter the one person who asked for details. Craig did not have a blog of any kind, let alone one about local history.

Safely ensconced in his room, he sat on the bed and took stock of the situation. He'd checked his phone a few times and did it again, but Stark had not replied. With no ghosts to question and no updates on the mysterious partner, he wondered what his next move should be. In movies, the action hero always knew what to do next. Craig, who was not an action hero in a movie, had no idea about his next moves. So, he turned on the TV and drank some coffee.

Not exactly James Bond, he thought. *Or even Austin Powers.*

He decided to take a shower, which was, at least, an action of some kind. As always, feeling jets of warm water cascade over him let Craig think more freely. He recalled an old Buddhist saying.

In difficult circumstances, there may be some useful action that can be performed. If not, gather information. If no information is available, sleep.

He was not sure of the exact wording, but he supposed it was translated anyway.

The point, he thought, as he toweled himself off, *is to get more data on Grendon Mill. The library and the church are obvious places to start. Somebody must know something.*

Feeling cleaner and with a small caffeine boost perking him up, Craig checked his phone again. Stark had finally replied. As was typical, the middleman was cagey.

T. will approach you. Go somewhere public.

Craig took the stairs down two floors to the lobby. As he left the hotel, he almost collided with someone. It was the tall, dark-haired woman from the bus station who had been engrossed in her phone. The two of them reeled back and Craig almost fell. The woman, laughing with embarrassment, grabbed him by the arm. She had a very strong grip and set him upright.

"Oh God, I'm so sorry. I'm always doing that."

"No problem," Craig replied, feeling stupid and wary.

Had an odd tingling sensation run up his arm? It had passed in a moment, but he was almost sure the woman's touch had a disturbingly familiar feel. Almost like being touched by a ghost. Up close, he could see that she was in her mid-forties, perhaps older, with a firm set to her mouth. She was appraising him with keen brown eyes. She had a hint of a West Coast accent.

"You're Craig," she said, lowering her voice. "The ghost whisperer, right?"

"Um—right, so you must be Tara?"

She nodded, glancing around. A young couple approached across the hotel parking lot. They would soon be within earshot.

"Stark sent me a picture," she explained. "Probably best if we act like a couple meeting up here?"

Craig asked her what the plan was while trying to look like her boyfriend, a hasty improvisation.

"Walk with me," she said, smiling back. "Stark told me to get you up to speed. Then we can go relic hunting."

They passed the young couple, who checked their phones, each seemingly oblivious to the other's existence. Once they were in the clear, Tara asked if he'd gleaned anything since this morning. He explained why he hadn't.

"A ghost shortage? That's a new one," she mused.

A thought occurred to Craig.

"Do you think there's some connection to this amulet thing? I mean, the lack of ghosts?"

Tara looked surprised, then shrugged.

"Could be. All I know is, this weird cult back in the seventies was up to no good, and they all died in a fire. There was some talk of demonic activity, but my sources are pretty vague."

"Demonic?" Craig looked around as if a demon would suddenly pop up from behind a fence.

Seeing his expression, Tara laughed.

"There's no reason to think we're facing anything but one difficult ghost," she reassured him. "Between us, we've got the talents to deal with it."

Craig tried to smile confidently, but the word "demon" had shaken him. He knew enough about the so-called lower beings to never want to encounter one. Wanting to change the subject, he talked about visiting the library and church.

Tara agreed that was sensible, then pointed out that, as a woman, it might be easier for her to talk to the locals.

"If we carry on the pretense of being a couple, it would make things easier," she explained. "We can visit stores, look at knick-knacks, talk to the staff. Let's work out our game plan."

Tara led him to a bench by the fountain, where they faked some laughter and general joking around. She laid her hand on his a couple of times, and he felt that odd sensation again. After the second time, a disturbing thought occurred to him. He asked her what her paranormal talent was.

"You know about me," he pointed out. "Stark never told me what your ability was."

"Cards on the table," she said. "I'm a reader. A telepath, if you like. It's very mild. I need physical contact to get even surface thoughts. That's why I bumped into you, to make sure you were who I thought."

Craig nodded, then looked down at the back of his hand.

"Sorry," she said, following his glance. "I wasn't peeking this time, I promise. That was just acting to fool other people. The point is, we complement each other. I can interact with the living and know what they really think, what they truly know. You can pump the dead for information. I can't read ghosts—it's too vague, like trying to catch hold of smoke."

A thought seemed to strike her, and she took out her phone.

"Stark sent me a picture of you, but it's not very good. That's why I had to make sure."

She fiddled with the screen for a moment then held it up for him to see. The photo was indeed poor quality, showing Craig smiling lopsidedly and looking self-conscious. It was taken from his ghost tours page on Facebook. He could see why Tara had felt the need to make sure of his identity.

"Yeah, that is pretty poor," he admitted. "He should've just taken a snapshot of me in the pub last night. So, what's the plan, partner?"

Tara looked around, then back at Craig.

"I've already got something—well, maybe. Did you notice, back at the hotel, that they had those little leaflets? The local places of interest, that kind of stuff?"

Craig had glanced through a couple when he'd checked in.

"You think there's a clue there?"

Tara leaned a little closer and lowered her voice.

"Sometimes, the absence of information gives things away. Those leaflets advertise the museum, talk about old houses, and the rowboats you can hire on the river. There's stuff about neighboring towns, too. But what's missing?"

Craig frowned in thought, looking around them. Nothing leaped out. All he could see were the houses, the public buildings, the fountain, and a war memorial. He gazed up Main Street toward the outskirts of town, where the road vanished into a vast expanse of gray-green, hazy in the distance.

"The woods!" he almost shouted.

Tara put a hand on his arm to quiet him.

"Right," she said. "Nothing about hiking or nature trails or wildlife. The river, yeah. They offer boat rides. But the woods seem to be off-limits. I mentioned hiking in passing to the guy at reception. He said something evasive about snakes and swampy ground. Then I fumbled with my purse and dropped some stuff on the counter, so he naturally helped me pick it up. I brushed his hand. It was enough."

Craig stared at her, impressed by how much she'd accomplished in the few hours since they'd arrived.

"What do you think I saw?" Tara asked.

"He was—I don't know—scared of the woods, maybe?"

"He was!" she said as if Craig were a child. "Nobody goes to the woods."

Craig pondered that, looking again at the distant expanse of forest.

"That's a lot of terrain to search for one small object. Or a ghost."

"Yeah," Tara said, "but suppose it's the ghost of the amulet that's scaring people off? Aren't there places where ghosts give off this bad vibe, kind of attack people's minds? Induce panic and fear?"

Craig felt more comfortable with this line of conversation. He was back on familiar ground.

"Yeah," he said. "They can do a whole bunch of stuff. Induce fear and panic, but also confuse and disorient people. They can even deceive people into making fatal mistakes—like walking off a cliff, that kind of thing."

"Exactly," Tara said. "I'll bet a hostile ghost is keeping people away from that amulet, so we seek out the dead guy, and you win him over."

Craig felt this was a somewhat optimistic assessment and said so. He felt they should do some more research into the area in case the woods were disliked for another reason. And he noted that the woods covered many square miles, so wandering about aimlessly seemed a little inefficient, if not futile.

"What if there are snakes? Or swampy ground?" he pointed out. "We're kind of in the boondocks here. Hell, there might even be bears."

Tara narrowed her eyes, and for a moment, Craig wondered if she was going to try and boss him around. But then her expression cleared.

"Yeah, you're right. Always get as much data as you can. Tell you what, we'll split up to cover more ground. I'll wander into some of these cute little mom-and-pop stores, and you check out the church and the library. Also, let's swap phone numbers."

CHAPTER 6

HITTING THE BOOKS

The combined library and museum was closer, so Craig went there first. Inside, he found a single large room under an impressive glass dome that added to the light streaming in through the high windows. Each window had a small strip of colored glass at the bottom with a pattern of five-petaled flowers.

Red roses, Craig thought. It made for a nice effect, casting little splashes of red onto the otherwise drab carpeting.

A handful of people browsed bookshelves or carousels. At a table, a man was absorbed in a newspaper, the top of his nearly bald head visible. The man looked up. It was the old guy from the fountain. He gave Craig a look that did not invite further conversation. Then, he resumed his scrutiny of the paper.

A neatly dressed woman stood behind a desk near the entrance. She looked like a librarian from central casting, complete with horn-rimmed spectacles dangling on a chain and graying hair pulled back into a severe bun. Her name badge read HETTIE LONSDALE, SENIOR LIBRARIAN, which had a suitably Victorian feel. But when Craig walked over to her, she smiled warmly and didn't bother lowering her voice when she greeted him.

"Hmm, our first tourist of the season. Welcome to our little town."

"Thank you," Craig replied. "I'm looking for some information on local history, stuff like that?"

"Ah, that's good to hear. Let me show you our little history section. Did you just get into town, Mister…?"

"Ellison. Craig Ellison."

After he'd given his name, he wondered if he should have lied. But in a small town, how hard would it be for a nosy person to get his name from the hotel clerk? He had paid at the diner with a credit card, so that was another source of information. Lying made no sense. Honesty sometimes was the best policy.

"Pleased to meet you, Craig. I guess you're from the big city?" Hettie went on.

"Well, a city, anyhow," he smiled. "Not so big as all that. But I must say, this here is a refreshing change."

He felt sure she would see through him, but Hettie just beamed again.

"Oh, I'm so glad you like our little town. Now, along here we have some official history books. They have more to do with the entire county, really, but our town is mentioned. All a little dry, I'm afraid."

Craig looked at three dog-eared volumes that were clearly decades old, and a couple of newer paperbacks with faded covers.

"Is there anything on folklore? Local legends?"

It was hard to be sure, even in such good light, but the librarian's benign expression seemed to falter for a split second.

"Of course. But there's not much. Again, it's more about the county as a whole. I guess Grendon Mill has a rather dull history."

She glanced back at her desk, where an elderly lady had just placed a small stack of books.

"I'd better go deal with Mrs. Doody. She's got to have her fix of true crime."

Craig took a selection of volumes and sat at a table. It soon became apparent that, when it came to local history, you could judge a book by its cover. There were accounts of working in a lumber mill, and some fragments of social history, but nothing that hinted at strange events. Craig checked the indexes in desperation, but there was no reference to amulets or ghosts.

That brought him up short. He checked through the books again, running his finger down each index. G—no ghosts. Nor did he find any reference to hauntings under H. He wondered what people in Grendon Mill did for Halloween. He'd never liked Halloween but knew it was great fun for most youngsters.

Maybe the kids here just walk around being totally rational, he thought wryly. *And get no candy because it's bad for their teeth.*

A town with no visible ghosts was weird enough. A town without ghost stories, without a single haunted house or spooky anecdote was downright disturbing. Stark had not mentioned any of this. Craig went through the books again, this time looking for references to the woods. He found out that they were called "The Woods", which suggested a serious lack of imagination. The trees had provided raw materials for the sawmill back in the day. And that was it.

"What are you looking for?"

Craig jumped and twisted around in his chair. The voice had hissed in his ear, but nobody was nearby. Apart from Hettie at the desk, the only person he could see was the man reading the newspaper, who looked up again and gave him another cold stare. Craig felt his face grow hot with embarrassment.

"What are you looking for?"

This time, the voice was accompanied by a chill that made him yelp. It was as if an icicle was jabbed into the base of his skull. He stood up in a sudden panic, almost knocking over his chair. The old guy glared at him in disapproval. The librarian peered at him over her reading glasses.

Craig turned around slowly, determined to find the ghost. Normally, he had no problem making contact with the dead, but this was strange. It felt wrong. Some ghosts were intrinsically mischievous or even aggressive. Craig was patient back home, cajoling, and good-humored with challenging spirits. It worked most of the time. He was on unfamiliar ground here, though.

He picked up the books and replaced them on the shelf. He then set out to conceal himself in one of the aisles. If he was going to talk to a ghost, he needed to be out of sight of the living. Then, he noticed the aisle he had picked happened to be True Crime, and that most of the books dealt with real-life horrors. It did nothing for his confidence to see titles like *The Butcher of Baltimore* and *Cannibal Families of the Appalachians*.

Focus, Craig, he told himself and cleared his throat. Then, he whispered into the shadows.

"I'm looking for an amulet."

At first, he thought there would be no response. But then, the far end of the aisle grew dark as if a black cloud had obscured the afternoon sun. It was not a shadow, though, or at least not a normal one. A vague form, elongated and writhing, came into view and drifted toward him.

"Oh, God," he breathed.

He'd seen hundreds of ghosts, but never one like this. It was not shaped like a normal human being, and he could make out only a few details, no hint of a face other than a vague oval blur. The entity moved like a column of dense smoke, silent and deceptive, suddenly vanishing, and materializing again a moment later just a few feet away. The face grew slightly clearer, two dark holes that must be eyes, a greater oval below them opening wider than any mouth had a right to.

"No! No! Don't look, never seek. Keep away. Searching is forbidden! Don't snoop, or you'll be sorry."

The thing's voice rose from a hiss to a shriek. It swirled toward him, grotesquely long fingers reaching to enclose his face. Flinching, Craig backed away, banging his shoulder against a shelf, dislodging a couple of books that hit the gray carpet with startling thuds. The shadowy hands clutched at him, and he covered his face. He felt vicious cold start to penetrate his fingers, and then the flesh of his cheeks.

"What is going on here?"

The freezing sensation vanished as suddenly as it had begun. Craig was sprawled on the floor next to the True Crime aisle with the librarian standing over him, arms akimbo. Farther away, the old man was just visible, heading for the exit.

"Really, young man, this is no way to behave in a library."

"I… I guess not," Craig said. "But I just saw—something. A ghost. You didn't see it?"

Hettie's expression grew sterner.

"I have no idea what you are talking about, but I suspect you have been taking something. Let us hope it is prescription medication."

Craig had heard variations on that theme so many times that he didn't bother arguing. People determined not to believe in something could not be convinced. Or—and this seemed more likely—people in haunted buildings were sometimes in denial. Challenging that only made them upset.

"I'm sorry. And I'm not on drugs of any kind," he said, rubbing his bruised shoulder. "I just had a fright. Guess I'm jumping at shadows."

Relenting somewhat, Hettie reached down and helped him up.

"Perhaps this is not the place for you," she said.

Taking the hint, Craig left. Outside, he got a surprise. The old guy he'd met at the fountain was waiting. At first, Craig expected another angry outburst. But instead, the man looked concerned. He took Craig by the lapel of his coat and whispered urgently.

"Do not rock the boat, son. They see most everything that happens around here, and they have ways…"

"Who? Who do you mean?" Craig asked.

But the old man was already scurrying away, head down. Craig thought back to their first encounter and remembered the guy's face. What he had assumed was anger back then—had it been fear? Perhaps terror at the mere mention of ghosts?

CHAPTER 7

CHURCHGOING

Something was seriously wrong with that ghost. Deformed. Deranged. Just plain wrong.
Craig kept turning the thought over in his head as he walked back to the
fountain and then paused to ponder his next move. He could hardly go
back to the library. Was it possible that he'd encountered a ghost that could
kill him? It was a disturbing thought. Not least because he couldn't think
of a way to find out. Other than the hard way.

The church caught his attention. It was a pleasant-looking building, if
rather bland in design. He decided to see if the local clergy could help. A
religious leader might be more forthcoming about the supernatural. Surely,
the kind of experience he'd just had could not be unique.

A text pinged on his phone. It was Tara, telling him she'd found
nothing so far. He had forgotten her in his confusion. He texted back.

> *Ghost in library. Might be dangerous, warned me off. Trying church*
> *next.*

He waited for a reply but put his phone away when he did not get one
after a minute, walked across the square, and paused at the church
noticeboard.

The name of Grendon Mill's sole place of worship struck him as odd.
The First Reformed Church of the Radiant Truth. There was no legal
requirement to mention God—or any god or saint—in a church's name.
But it seemed a little off to Craig, who was raised Episcopalian. Still, small
towns often harbored curious little sects, and he shouldn't judge. He

looked more closely at the notice board. There were meetings, fundraising for local charities, and an appeal for funds to fix the roof. All unsurprising.

Then, he noticed something else. Where were the service times? Normally, a church noticeboard was quite clear on when you were supposed to turn up for the religious stuff. Nothing of that sort here. But of course, Craig told himself, that information might be inside the building.

Only one way to find out.

A small graveyard held a handful of headstones, all dating back to the Victorian era or early twentieth century. Craig paused to read some of the names. He saw a couple of Hallorans from the 1900s, presumably the police chief's ancestors. Moving along a row, he saw Bradley, Green, Foster, and Carmichael, but no Grendon. That seemed odd. Perhaps the Grendon family was of a different denomination?

"It's a very civilized pastime, I always feel."

Craig looked up from a weathered tombstone to see a short, round-faced man of about fifty looking back at him. The stranger wore a clerical collar and a dark suit.

"Sorry?"

"The epitaphs, dates, et cetera," the minister said. "Reading them is so relaxing. Puts things into perspective, doesn't it?"

The short man held out a hand.

"I'm Paul Foster," he explained. "I minister to the little congregation here."

Craig gave him his name and took the hand, which was cool and a little damp. He had to resist the urge to wipe his hand on his pants after they'd shaken.

They talked some more, and Craig found himself warming a little to the minister. Foster had precise, bird-like mannerisms and spoke with enthusiasm about the church, its history, and the town in general. He ushered Craig inside and invited him to admire the stained-glass windows, which dated back to the foundation of Grendon Mill.

"Of course," Foster added, "they have been repaired a few times."

The windows were interesting in that they all consisted of geometric patterns. As with the name of the church, there seemed to be no reference to God or any Biblical characters. Instead, each window was emblazoned with interlocking patterns that slightly bewildered the eye. Along the bottom of each pane of glass was a row of stars, set against a red-and-blue-striped background. At the top of each window was a word that seemed to have vague religious connotations. They were large enough to read easily. Five windows on each side of the church bore the same words.

LIFE. POWER. FAITH. MYSTERY. TRUTH.

"Very impressive," Craig mused. "But also, very different from other churches I've seen."

The minister nodded enthusiastically as if it was a compliment.

"Ah yes, the windows are pure of any image. Pictures of people, however holy, can be distracting, whereas abstract patterns are conducive to meditation. Or so we like to think."

Craig was not sure how much he should disclose to the little man. He decided to fence a little.

"So, you're a bit like the Quakers, perhaps? I don't see any crucifixes or other Christian symbols."

Foster clapped his hands in pleasure.

"Yes. Most astute. We focus on the spiritual aspects of religion. I know that sounds a little absurd—aren't all faiths spiritual? But we believe true enlightenment comes from within, that a human being must cultivate their soul through meditation and inward contemplation."

"And you've been in Grendon Mill since it was founded?"

"Quite so," confirmed the minister.

Craig hesitated, then asked why there were no Grendon graves in the churchyard. Again, Foster was pleased.

"How very observant of you!" he exclaimed. "Yes, the Grendons were Catholic, and there was originally a small chapel. But the Grendon family sadly died out some while back, and the chapel fell into disuse. It was torn down long before my time."

"So, yours is the only church now," Craig said, looking up at the nearest window.

The abstract patterns might have adorned the window of a fancy hotel or an Art Deco office building. To Craig, they didn't speak of religion. They proclaimed nothing at all.

"Yes, we're the only game in town," the minister confirmed. "A pity, in a way. It would be nice to be part of a wider ecumenical community."

"Why is it called the Church of the Radiant Truth?" Craig asked.

"Truth is a spiritual light," Foster replied. "Sometimes, it is so bright that it might blind those who seek it. And thus, truth seekers might go astray and need help to return to the right path."

Craig thought it was the perfect evasive answer. It sounded religious and benevolent but meant nothing too specific. He had often felt that about preachers of all kinds. It didn't prove Foster was up to something. And as Craig had struck out at the library, the church seemed the last resort.

"I have another question, and I apologize if it's offensive," Craig said. "Do you believe in ghosts?"

Foster's expression showed puzzlement, real or feigned, Craig wasn't sure.

"Ghosts? Well, that's a complex question. If you mean, do souls exist independently of the flesh, the answer is an emphatic yes. But we do not claim to know the place or purpose of such souls."

"Yes," Craig said, "but I'm talking about actual ghosts—the souls of the dead that linger on the mortal plane, kind of. You see, I run a ghost tour, so that kind of thing interests me. Hauntings and such."

Foster tilted his head and raised an eyebrow.

"A ghost tour? Well, that's interesting. But I'm afraid there are no haunted houses around here, no legends of headless horsemen, or anything of that sort. I don't think you'll find many ghosts in Grendon Mill."

Craig sighed. It was the answer he'd expected, but it was still disappointing. He had now asked three locals about ghosts. In a small town, it was likely that word would get around quickly and draw unwanted attention. He thought again of the rival investigators Stark had mentioned, and the hard-bitten stranger outside Hannigan's. If that guy was the opposition, Craig might be in serious trouble. Still, he wasn't alone, and Tara seemed efficient.

"Is there anything else…?"

Foster left the question dangling. Craig had been lost in thought and was flustered by how easily he'd forgotten the little man's presence.

"Oh, no, Reverend, I've taken enough of your time."

The minister laughed.

"Nobody has ever called me Reverend," he said. "You know, I kind of like it. Must be fun to be revered."

Craig left the church and texted Tara the bad news. She replied instantly.

Meet me outside the tackle store.

CHAPTER 8
SUDDEN CHANGE OF PLAN

Craig didn't recall a tackle store but asked a passerby who quickly set him right. The place in question was half-hidden around a corner, just off the town square. Tara was outside, checking her phone.

"Hi honey," she said loudly enough to be overheard.

She took him by the elbow and steered him away from people lingering outside the store.

"You been pricing fishing rods?" he asked.

"Not my idea of fun," she said in a low voice. "But don't you think it's interesting? A store catering to fishermen, but nothing for hunters. I checked inside. No guns, Bowie knives, crossbows, any of that stuff."

"Nothing related to the woods," Craig said. "I get it. The woods are verboten."

They exchanged more information, Craig giving details of his encounters with the librarian and the minister but focusing mainly on the ghost. Tara asked some questions about the latter, but Craig struggled to be helpful. Beyond 'it was weird and scary', there wasn't much more to say.

"Except," he mused, "that it seemed… deformed, somehow. Like it was out of focus or distorted. A caricature of a ghost, almost. All the ghosts I've seen resembled the people they were in life. Some had injuries, of course, but most were just regular humans at first glance. This one was… monstrous. And it seemed a little crazy. Damaged in body and mind, except it has no body."

Tara pondered that for a few moments as they strolled across the square.

"So, we've found precisely one ghost, and it's weird. This amulet is a magical artifact. Could it be that the amulet is affecting that ghost?"

Craig hadn't thought of that, but it was an interesting idea.

"I've never known a ghost like it," he said slowly. "But I've never encountered a magical item before, either. Perhaps the ghost is affected by the amulet's power. It was definitely warning me off, so maybe it's guarding the amulet?"

Tara nodded vigorously.

"Proximity to arcane energy can affect living people—send them crazy, make them see visions. If the ghost is haunting the area around the amulet, who knows what harm it might do to the ghost? It would explain the distortion and the craziness."

Another thought struck Craig.

"What if the ghost's haunted item is the amulet?"

Seeing Tara's puzzlement, he went on.

"A ghost always haunts something, usually a specific material object associated with their death."

Understanding dawned on Tara's face.

"Ah, yeah, like the bullet that killed them. Or a sword, maybe."

Craig smiled. He would have suggested something milder like a favorite book or toy.

"That's right. So, if a person died while holding the amulet, or wearing it, they could be attached to it. Anchored to it. And its power might affect them in all sorts of strange ways."

Tara looked impressed.

"That's a cool theory. Let's put the pieces together. First, the woods are scary, and the locals don't go there. Second, no normal ghosts in Grendon Mill. Third, a weird ghost warned you off in the library. And we know a ghost can't stray far from its haunted item."

She gestured at the woods in the distance. Craig saw what she was hinting at.

"So, the ghost might be at the limit of its range, and therefore…"

"Precisely. Let's look at a map."

They took a seat on a bench, and she took out her phone. Google Earth provided a satellite view of the town and a handy scale. If a ghost was based in the woods, and its radius of action included the library, it narrowed down the search area, but not by a lot. It was at least a square mile of forest. And that was assuming the phantom Craig had seen was linked to the amulet in the first place. It was still all highly speculative, he reminded her.

"Sometimes," Tara said, putting away her phone, "you've got to play your hunches. I think we should go for a walk in the woods before sundown."

She looked at Craig's sneakers.

"I've got some walking boots. Do you?"

He didn't and felt stupid. Why hadn't he thought about hiking gear when he agreed to go to a rural area?

"I'll be okay," Craig said. "It's not like we're exploring the Amazon jungle, right?"

Tara looked hesitant but said nothing. They returned to their hotel so she could change her footwear and then headed along the road toward the woods. Tara talked in general about the amulet as they walked, admitting she didn't know what it looked like.

"Either Stark doesn't know," she said, "or he's being too damn secretive about it."

Craig was happy to badmouth his employer and did so for a few enjoyable minutes. It was a way to distract himself from the looming mass of trees ahead. The ghost in the library had left him worried and confused, but he had to try to communicate. That first encounter had been a surprise, but he was prepared now. Whatever the entity's problem was, he would try and help.

It's what I do, Craig thought. *It's my job, my vocation. I help the dead. I'm not irrationally scared of them.*

The icy sting of the ghost's touch was still fresh in his mind, though. He had seen ghosts kill. He had, at Stark's behest, even urged them to end the lives of evil people. What if someone else was manipulating the ghost he'd seen in the library? The thought was as unwelcome as it was credible. He shared the idea with Tara.

"Maybe," she said. "But let's not invent problems for ourselves, okay? If this amulet is still hidden, it seems unlikely that the ghost haunting it is under anyone's control, right?"

"Right."

That reassured Craig. He started to rehearse the ways he might open a dialogue with the ghost, reviewing his past successes. He'd encountered some hostile ones, a few who had raged at the world and threatened Craig. But the simple fact that he would listen to them tended to defuse their anger, at least to some degree.

Craig's musings were interrupted by a slight ping. He had received a text or an email. It might be Stark offering some useful information for a change. Tara had fallen silent and was focused on the road ahead. Feeling glad to have an experienced partner in this weird quest, he took out his phone and thumbed in the password. It was a text, but not from Stark. It was from an unknown number.

Craig hesitated and then opened the message.

Hey, Craig, I'm at Dinah's Diner. Let's meet up. T.

Craig stared at the words, desperately trying to interpret them in some way that wasn't disastrous. Of course, he couldn't. There was an odd roaring sound in his ears, like the sound of the sea in a gathering storm.

Surely, "T" is for Tara?

The woman at his side stopped walking and, before he could react, laid a cool hand on Craig's cheek. Then she shook her head sadly.

"Oh Craig, you are so dumb. But I like you."

"What... who the hell..."

"I could lie," the woman said. "Tell you that's a message from an impostor. But you'd be unsure, wouldn't you? Best we keep things honest from now on."

"Gee, thanks," Craig said. "I'd hate for there to be any confusion."

The false Tara smiled. Now that he knew what she was, that smile had a distinctly predatory look. She suddenly reminded Craig of an ex-girlfriend who had cleaned out his bank account and vanished with most of his stuff. This time, he had a feeling he was about to lose something far more significant.

"No need to be upset, Craig," the woman said. "I need your help, and I'm prepared to cut you in on the deal. I have a client who can pay a lot more than that slimeball Stark. Not a middleman, but a collector. A very wealthy one. And you could be very rich very soon. You could say goodbye to that crummy town, the lame ghost tours, Stark, all that crap. Start a new life. What do you think? Help me get the amulet, and we'll split the fee, seventy-thirty. And I'll put you in touch with my employer if you like. He's always on the lookout for fresh talent. What about it, Craig? Come on. It's the chance of a lifetime."

Craig hesitated, and it wouldn't take a telepath to see he was wavering. He owed Stark nothing, but he was sure the middleman had considerable reach and would not forgive or forget betrayal. And why should he trust this woman, who had lied her way into his life?

"No," he said. "No deal. I'm going back to Grendon Mill, and you can..."

The fake Tara shook her head.

"No, Craig. You're not going anywhere without my say-so."

He half expected her to hit him, followed by the shameful thought that she might beat him in a fight. He took a step back, unsure of whether to run or face her down. The woman reached into her jacket and took out a gun. The afternoon sunlight glinted off the metal. The false Tara thumbed back the hammer and aimed at his chest. It was something Craig had seen done many times on TV. It felt very different in real life.

"Now, we do it old-school." There was no hint of cajolery in her voice now, and her dark eyes were hard as flints.

"Now, we get off the road. We're going into the woods. And you're going first."

CHAPTER 9
DARK AND DEEP

"You'll never get away with this."

Even as he said the words, Craig felt they were a pretty feeble comeback.

"I've already gotten away with it, Craig," she said. "You will cooperate, or I will shoot you dead and leave your body for the crows, or whatever the hell eats dead bodies out here."

Craig stumbled ahead of her, a spot between his shoulder blades starting to itch. In fewer than twenty-four hours, he had gone from getting paid for an "easy job" to this. He had no doubt this woman would shoot him and leave him to rot, maybe conceal his body under some branches, that kind of thing. He'd seen it done in the movies so many times. He could imagine the possible variations—two in the body, one in the head. The gun muzzle against his skull, execution-style. Perhaps make him dig his own grave beforehand?

Probably not. We don't have any tools for that...

He stumbled over a root and fell heavily, his hands sinking into leaf mulch.

"Watch where you're going, Craig. And if that's an attempt to trick me, it's feeble."

He got up, brushing the gunk from his hands onto his jeans, then regretting the mess it made.

As if it mattered. Whether or not they found the amulet, this was the end of the road for Craig Ellison.

He walked on, numb now, wondering if men on death row felt like this. The despair and fear and panic were gone. He felt nothing. He even began to wonder, on a purely intellectual level, if he would haunt these woods or move on. If the latter, where would he go?

He stumbled again but didn't fall this time. They were deep in the woods now. A faint blare of a car horn underlined how far behind the road was, and with that, all hope of rescue.

"No ghosts yet, Craig?"

A hand gripped his shoulder, and he felt the tingling sensation. She had to make contact to skim his thoughts, make sure he wasn't holding out on her. Which put her within reach…

A vicious blow struck him on the back of the neck, and he was on his knees again.

"Don't even think about it, you moron."

It was like being told not to think of a pink elephant, but he did his best. He got up and didn't bother wiping the dirt from his hands this time. Why bother? There was no way out. She kept gripping his shoulder with the gun shoved into his back. He had to tell the truth. There was nothing to tell, though.

"We'll just have to keep looking, won't we?" she said.

There was no sound for a few minutes, apart from the crackle of dried vegetation shoved aside or crushed underfoot. Then, he heard it. Or rather, them.

It was a faint wailing sound, rising and falling, sometimes just on the edge of perception. Voices. Human, perhaps.

"More than one, huh?" the false Tara asked. "Well, you'll just have to be extra persuasive. One of them must know where the damned amulet is."

The sound grew louder. He could distinguish individual voices and a few random syllables now. There were words amid the wailing. Craig could not make them out, but he could hear laughter and weeping, a disturbing mixture. He thought of the ghost in the library, its wild words and distorted form. He imagined a host of such entities and shuddered.

"Don't be such a wuss," the woman snarled, pulling him to a halt. "Let's wait for them to come to us."

Craig stood still, the bruising on his back from the gun muzzle a throbbing patch of discomfort. It occurred to him that the ghosts might not be pleased to see him held captive by a killer.

"Good point," she said.

She spun him around and shoved the small pistol back into her jacket pocket.

"Now, we play the happy couple again. Just stay focused on the mission."

Craig hardly heard her. He was staring past her left shoulder at a figure just a few paces behind her. He almost laughed despite the situation.

The newcomer was dressed so poorly that he made Stark look debonair. Clashing colors, an open shirt with a medallion hanging amid abundant chest hair—of course, it was a ghost. No living man would look like that unless he was acting in a movie about the seventies. Or perhaps it was a dare.

The woman grabbed his right hand with her left, letting go almost at once. The ghost had disappeared by the time she'd spun around, but not before giving a shake of the head that, Craig felt, had a touch of finality about it.

"Where the hell—"

The woman was caught off-guard. Craig seized the moment without thinking and flung himself onto her, a clumsy attack that knocked her down with him sprawled diagonally on top of her. The gun went off somehow, and the sound was deafening. The woman gasped and thrashed. For a moment, he hoped she'd shot herself.

He froze. It was a mistake. She drove an elbow into his side and then flung him sideways and got to her knees. The gun was out again and aimed at his face.

"You jerk," she grated. "I'll give you one more—"

The ghosts appeared all around them, shifting skeins of darkness as if the shadows under the trees had come alive. Patches of gray became faces of a sort. The wailing was louder now, coupled with laughter and manic outbursts of semi-coherent speech.

The woman stopped glaring at Craig and looked around her.

"Oh, Jesus," she breathed.

Craig had no idea if she could see the ghosts, but she certainly saw something. She scrambled to her feet as one danced a zigzag path toward her. A dark limb reached out. The moment the elongated fingers touched her head, the woman screamed and reeled to one side. Now, the ghosts were more substantial. There were eight or nine—it was hard to tell—that circled or darted back and forth. Paralyzed by shock, Craig tried to make sense of what some of them were saying, but it was a crazy jumble.

"The woods are lovely, dark, and deep…"

"Bad people, coming here…"

"So much pain, oh so much pain!"

"Help me, help me!"

"The Five command, the reapers of my soul, oh my soul!"

A face appeared just inches in front of Craig. The features were better defined this time, and even in his fear, he felt a thrill of recognition.

A chubby girl, smiling in a photo. Someone had shown him that picture on a phone.

"You have a cute cat," he blurted out.

The ghost reacted with an almost comical surprise: mouth opening to an impossible size, eyes growing into vast dark pools. Then some borderline human features returned, and the mouth emitted a plaintive wail.

"Binky! I miss Binky!"

The ghost wandered away, pining for her pet. Craig got up slowly, raising a hand in what he hoped was a friendly gesture.

"Guys, I can see and hear you. I'm here to help."

There was a moment's silence. Then came laughter, sounding even more deranged, accompanied by curses, threats, teasing, and mocking. The fake Tara was still on the ground, looking around her with wild eyes, the gun no longer aimed at Craig.

Three ghosts closed in on her. One emitted piercing shrieks and pranced back and forth. Suddenly, it stooped and plunged its malformed fingers into her head.

The woman's screams rivaled those of the ghosts. She dropped the gun and rolled in the undergrowth, her hands clamped to her skull. Three ghosts shrieked with laughter around her. Then, they closed in and began to play with their prey, poking and tickling in a horrible parody of a childish game. Most of the others joined in. The woman got to her feet somehow and started to run, only to be brought down in seconds, twitching and howling.

Sickened, Craig turned to run back the way they'd come, but a ghost blocked his path. It was smaller and more compact than the others. It seemed conflicted, whimpering, not quite coming within reach.

He backed away until he was up against a tree trunk, all the while talking rapidly.

"I can help you move on. Tell me your story, and you can leave this plane and go somewhere better, where you won't suffer anymore—"

"Suffer."

The ghost came closer, reaching out for him with shadowy arms.

"The Five, they say we've all got to suffer."

"I can help you. Let me help!" Craig cried.

The ghost stopped, its outline rippling.

"Help?"

It was a girl's voice, perhaps a teenager. The face was clearer now, and not just the face. Above it was a hint of color, electric blue, conspicuous against the dark green of the woods. It triggered another memory.

"Nikki? Is that you? Chloe still misses you."

"Chloe? Chloeeeee!"

The girl began to writhe, advancing then retreating, crying out in torment. Behind her, the fake Tara crawled slowly, collapsed, and then got back up on all fours. The ghosts would soon be done with her.

Craig ran, weaving between trees, leaping over fallen logs. There was no way he could deal with this. The ghosts were insane, malevolent, wrong in a way that terrified him.

After a while, the throbbing pain on his side slowed him to a fast walk. He looked back for the first time and saw no sign of pursuit. The trees began to thin out, and he expected to see the road again. Instead, the outskirts of Grendon Mill appeared ahead of him.

He started to run again, racing for the pastel-painted clapboard houses, expecting to feel the cold, deadly grip of the angry dead at any moment.

CHAPTER 10
THE OTHER WOMAN

Craig realized how messy he looked when he calmed down a little. He got quizzical looks from a few people as he made his way back to the center of town. He paused to look at himself in a store window and saw a wild-eyed, disheveled figure. His jeans were marred by smears of leaf mulch that also encased his shoes. His hands were filthy, and quite a bit of dirt had somehow migrated to his face.

Hair's still pretty neat, though, he thought ruefully. *Small victories.*

He promptly ran a hand through his hair and then swore. His hand shook badly. His mutilated toe had started to throb some time ago, but he'd been able to ignore it until now. He looked back at the woods, which were now partly obscured by a row of pleasant two-story houses.

A woman lay dead somewhere under that green ocean of leafage. He was sure the fake Tara could not have survived the ghosts' attack. He was just as certain that he could not have saved her. But he still felt guilty. There was no good way to die, but the woman had just suffered one of the worst deaths Craig had heard of.

"You been to the woods, boy?"

Craig almost collided with the old man from the fountain and the library. He was peering up at Craig in disapproval. There seemed to be little point in lying.

"Yes. Yes, I have."

The oldster crossed his arms, still looking at him. He had evidently expected more from Craig.

"It's—it's kind of big, isn't it?"

It was all he could think of saying, and the old man raised his eyebrows incredulously.

"Oh yeah, big. That's what strikes everybody about the woods," he snorted. "You young idiot. I warned you. Still, I guess some people just won't be told. On your own head be it."

Craig stared as the old man walked off down a side street, muttering querulously. Then he set off again, quickly reaching the town square. Craig cut across to Dinah's Diner but then hesitated. He scraped some dirt off his shoes onto the sidewalk and cleaned his face as best he could. He caught a glimpse of himself in the door as he pushed it open. He still looked like he'd been beaten up by the Swamp Thing.

A couple of waitstaff gave him an appraising look but said nothing. Chief Halloran was no longer around, which was a relief. It was late afternoon, and clearly a slack time. Only a few booths were occupied, and there was one woman on her own. She smiled at him and waved him over.

Is this the real Tara? Craig thought as he approached the booth. *Logically, it must be. But I was fooled once…*

The woman was petite, and in her mid- to late-twenties, with a pale complexion and short red hair. She was pretty, but there was a firm set to her mouth and slight shadows under her eyes.

"Hi, Craig," she said. "You been mudwrestling?"

"Kind of," he said, sliding in to sit opposite her.

Only after he'd slumped into the seat did he realize how exhausted he was. The stress of the encounter and his wild run through the trees had done a number on him. Tara signaled a waitress, and a cup of steaming coffee soon appeared in front of him.

"My friend here had a bit of a mishap," Tara told the waitress. "Fell into a ditch, right, Craig?"

He goggled at her, then managed to say, "Yeah."

"Men—they always think they're so practical, but he's such a klutz," Tara went on, beaming up at the waitress, who smiled back in feminine solidarity. "Oh, and can I have another piece of that pumpkin pie? It's just wonderful."

The waitress left, and Craig gulped down the coffee, scalding his tongue and throat. Then he leaned back, staring at his new... hopefully real partner in not-exactly crime.

"You look like..." she said, lowering her voice. "What the hell happened?"

He told her, in fragments at first, then settling down to get the details in the right order. Tara didn't seem surprised. When he finished, she picked up her phone and made a call.

"Hi, Perry? Got an update. Seems like a rival operative followed Craig and shadowed him here."

Craig stared as she brought Stark up to speed, keeping her voice low and covering her mouth with her free hand. It took Craig a few seconds to grasp that she was shielding herself from lipreaders. He'd never have thought of that. No wonder she enjoyed Stark's confidence. Tara was talking to their employer pretty much as an equal. Craig's frustration at hearing a one-sided conversation was offset by relief. Here was a competent person. She might know what to do next.

Tara signed off, laid down her phone, and smiled at Craig.

"Sorry, I didn't mean to be rude, but I thought I'd better check in. I'm glad you're okay. Now, let's go over things again. You'd be surprised how much you might have forgotten or left out. Why not start with when you met up with Stark yesterday?"

Craig, fueled by refills of good coffee, recalled every detail since the meeting in Hannigan's. Tara interrupted him for the first time when he got to the stranger at the pub. The description was familiar to her, and she asked to see the man's contact details. She then went into some kind of app on her phone and explained: "Misuse of the internet, very naughty."

She had a result a few moments later.

"Shane Ryan. I knew it."

The name meant nothing to Craig, and he said so.

"You've not been in this game for long, then," Tara said grimly. "I've never met him, but the guy has a solid reputation. Ryan's one of the most effective ghost hunters in North America, or at least New England. New Hampshire, I think, is his base of operations. But he has been known to range far and wide. He's not exactly predictable. Just very, *very* determined."

"So, he's a kind of gun for hire?" Craig asked. "He seemed very concerned about those missing kids."

Tara shrugged.

"I'm sure he is. He does a lot of white-knighting—rolls into town, beats the bad ghosts, and leaves. Clint Eastwood's got nothing on that guy. Are you sure one of the pictures he showed you was one of those crazy ghosts?"

Craig thought about it, forcing himself to relive the encounter.

"Yes, I'm sure. It was the girl with the cat. And not just the one this Ryan guy showed me. Another ghost was Nikki, Chloe's friend. So… those… those twisted things are what's left of kids who went missing? That means…"

He struggled with a swirling mass of ideas so hideous he desperately wanted none of them to be true. Tara spoke quietly.

"You think somebody is using these ghosts to create more of their kind? Kind of a self-perpetuating cycle?"

"Yes, that's what I think. Believe. Whatever."

He shuddered and passed a hand over his face. The sight of the impostor writhing under the ghosts' demented onslaught was still fresh in his mind. He wondered how long it might haunt his dreams. Or if he would ever forget it.

"Hey, take it easy, fella."

Tara reached out for his hand. He flinched, then apologized.

"I'm sorry," he said. "It's just the fake—the woman who said she was you—she worked by contact. And you never said what your talent is."

Tara leaned back and crossed her arms but took the sting out of the gesture with a cheeky smile.

"Guess. I'll give you a count of ten. Nine... eight... seven..."

Craig stared at her in puzzlement and then looked around the room. What power might she have that he could see? Nothing seemed different. People were chatting, working, eating. Clearly, Tara could not stop time.

"three... two..."

This is ridiculous, he thought. *Is she going to teleport herself to the ladies' room or something?*

He looked back at Tara, about to object to her game. Then he noticed that his coffee cup was rising into the air and turning slowly.

"Telekinesis," he said way too loudly.

Heads turned. The cup fell back onto the table, splashing coffee onto Craig's shirt. Tara rolled her eyes as she plucked some paper napkins from a holder and handed them to him.

"Okay, rookie, maybe we'd better get you back to the hotel so you can clean up. You did bring a change of clothes, right?"

Chapter 11
WASH DAY

The laundromat was not busy.

They sat side by side, watching Craig's clothes rotate in a swirl of foam. Occasionally, one of his sneakers hit the glass window with a muffled thud.

"Cheaper than Netflix," Tara remarked. "And when it's finally over, you don't feel you've wasted a few hours you'll never get back."

"How did you know this was even here?" Craig asked.

"You don't check to see if there's a laundromat when you go somewhere new? I always do," Tara replied. "Also, I scope out the eateries, coffee shops—the usual stuff. Always be prepared, like a good Girl Scout. Not that I ever was one."

Craig looked down at his clean socks, which were almost covered by an old pair of sweatpants. Along with the T-shirt he wore, they constituted his change of clothing. He made a mental note: *Be prepared*.

"It's been years since I went anywhere," he said. "God, I'm an idiot. I wasn't ready for this."

She looked up at him and then laid a hand on his arm.

"Don't beat yourself up over mistakes, false assumptions, or carelessness. One of the bravest and most intelligent men I've ever known used to do that."

"Thanks," he said. "This really brave man, is he anywhere nearby? And does he know about all this, you know... what you—we—do? Can he help us?"

Tara laughed, but it didn't reach her eyes. Craig had spent more time with ghosts than people for quite a while, but sadness looked much the same in the living as the dead.

"I don't know where he is. I can't contact him. But as he's probably in England, I don't think he'll be riding to the rescue."

"England? How did you two meet?" he asked.

"I went to college in London, then Cambridge. Astrophysics."

Craig's bafflement produced another burst of laughter.

"Your face!" she said. "Yeah, I'm a scientist. Or was. There's no money to be had, a bunch of grant-funding cuts across the board. NASA wasn't hiring. So here I am, freelancing as a paranormal investigator. Or whatever. I keep changing my job title."

Craig asked, tentatively, how a scientist ended up investigating the occult. Tara stared into the window of the washing machine and told him her story. How she'd survived an attack by werewolves that had killed her boyfriend. How this had led her to a man, a Cambridge professor called Marcus Mortlake, who had not only believed her but hunted down the beasts. And how further involvement with Mortlake had led to an unwelcome revelation about herself.

"Your psychic power?" Craig said, making sure he said it quietly this time.

"Yup," she said, still staring at the swirling clothes. "I guess I was in denial. When I was a kid, there were some issues with stones being thrown at our house. Everyone said it was just neighborhood kids messing around. But there were other things—noises, stuff moving inside the house. And that could've been me and my brother messing around, so nobody paid much attention to it."

"When did you find out the truth?"

"At a haunted house in England," she said quietly. "A friend asked me to help deal with it, and I asked Marcus, so we went. We had no idea what we were facing. The thing in that house took control of me and channeled the power I refused to believe I had. Somebody died because of it. My friend got hurt, too."

Her eyes were closed now. Craig laid a hand on hers, briefly and awkwardly, and dug for a few words of comfort. He wondered what the handful of other laundromat customers might think of these two strangers. Relationship issues? Maybe a breakup taking place during the spin cycle? He mentioned that and raised a smile.

"You got through that crisis," he went on. "And you can control your talent now, that's clear."

"Yeah, I control it most of the time," Tara said, looking up at him. "There's a reason they call them 'wild' talents. Gotta be in the zone. Telekinesis isn't much use against ghosts, or at least not directly. And from what you've told me, your friendly approach isn't going to win these ones over. So, we're stymied until we get more information because I have no idea what the hell is going on in this town. And not knowing important stuff really pisses me off."

She stretched out and yawned.

"I never thought I'd get bored talking about me, but here we are. Your turn. Tell me everything I need to know about Craig Ellison. And some things I don't to spice it up a little."

Craig talked, finding it easier than he'd expected. Tara didn't need convincing that the supernatural existed. He gave a condensed version of his life story. It was mostly a tale of a difficult childhood followed by drifting from place to place as an adult. Tara asked a few incisive questions, which became more frequent after the story reached Craig's first meeting with Peregrine Stark.

"He's a piece of work," she said. "He got you to persuade a ghost to kill people?"

"I guess," Craig said. "Billy spontaneously killed a guy during one of my ghost tours. That's how Stark came up with the idea."

Tara pondered that.

"Do you think Perry knew it would be a lot harder to get this amulet than he let on? Because he's a convoluted bastard. If we'd known it would be this tough, we might not have agreed to come at all, right?"

Craig had to agree. He had nearly died in the woods. He wondered aloud why the ghosts had focused on the fake Tara first rather than dividing to attack both intruders.

"Crazy ghosts doing crazy stuff, maybe," Tara said. "But it could be that, at some level, they sensed she was the enemy, and you weren't. Or… maybe they were ordered to do it. From what you said, this woman was pretty tough. She played hardball. That could make someone a priority target."

"You think the ghosts are under somebody's control?" he asked. "Hell, that's something else to worry about."

"Just a hypothesis," Tara said. "But I've encountered ghosts that were under the control of a demonic entity."

"A demon?" Craig whispered. "Oh, God."

"Just a possibility," Tara reassured him. "Probably not that at all. But we need to find out what makes these ghosts so weird. And ornery."

It was time to transfer Craig's stuff to the dryer. As they did so, a new customer came in. It was the old man with the service medals yet again. He saw Craig immediately and his expression changed from grumpy to offended.

"My nemesis just walked in," Craig whispered to Tara as they sat down again.

She didn't turn around, instead using her phone camera to look over her shoulder while pretending to check her hair and makeup. But she seemed to take a little longer with it than necessary just to peek at an old guy.

"The one who warned you off, right?"

He nodded. Tara stood.

"Let's see if my charms can succeed where yours failed."

Craig took out his phone to peek, watching Tara walk around the island of plastic seats and sit down by the old guy. He noticed her posture—half-turned toward the stranger, leaning forward, wide-eyed. She even fluttered her eyelashes a little. He couldn't hear what she said, but the pitch of her voice went up.

The old guy seemed as grumpy as ever, but Craig couldn't hear what he said. The man's back was to him. After a few moments, he seemed to be holding a conversation with Tara, who leaned a little closer and lowered her voice.

Well, he thought, *it wouldn't be the first time some old geezer fell for a young woman.*

He relaxed slightly and checked his laundry. The dryer thrummed away merrily, and the cycle was nearly done.

"Craig."

The voice that spoke his name was low and urgent. Craig looked around, but nobody was close enough to speak to him without yelling over the noise coming from the dryer.

"Craig, look out."

He saw movement in the round window of the dryer. Somebody stood outside the laundromat, looking in. A familiar figure, with a purple shirt open to show a medallion nestled in his chest hair. Craig had forgotten the fleeting sight amid the general confusion and fear. He had glimpsed the man for just a moment in the trees, behind the fake Tara. Moments before the crazy ghosts had claimed her.

And now, he was back.

CHAPTER 12
A SECOND SEER

Craig looked at his phone screen again, lifting and angling it to see the window clearly, to take a photo to show Tara. But no one stood outside, just a couple of kids walking past.

He twisted around in his seat. The man was still there, looking disturbingly like an extra from Saturday Night Fever. A second later, a middle-aged woman in an NYU sweatshirt walked right through him, hesitated, frowned, and then moved on out of sight.

A regular ghost, Craig thought. *One I could talk to…*

The figure disappeared as if the thought had banished him. But another ghost appeared at the same moment. One of the hideous, contorted things from the woods. It passed through a couple of cars as it crossed the street, a dark, not-quite-opaque parody of a human form. It zig-zagged, hesitated, and then retreated from the sidewalk for a moment. Then the dark ovals in the paler oval of its face seemed to fasten on the laundromat.

On Craig? No. On Tara and the old guy.

The grotesque phantom darted forward as Craig leaped up and shouted a warning. The ghost passed through the window and a washing machine then loomed over Tara, who stood and retreated along the row of seats. The ghost hovered in place as if deciding what to do next.

Craig heard its voice. A plaintive whine as if it was in pain.

"The Five command. I have no choice. Pity me…"

Tara couldn't see the ghost, but she sensed its rough location. A hand plunged into her coat pocket and pulled out something that gleamed.

"Where is it?" she shouted without looking at Craig.

"Just in front of the old man!" he yelled back.

The man seemed paralyzed by fear, but he was staring straight at the ghost. The old man was a seer, like Craig. That explained a lot.

Tara lashed out, and Craig realized she was using some kind of knuckleduster. Iron, presumably. The wide, swinging action took her hand through one of the ghost's too-long arms. The ghost flinched.

"A hit. It didn't like it!" Craig shouted.

"Did it disappear?" Tara asked.

"No. Move forward a little."

Tara wondered why iron did not have the intended effect. But she didn't hesitate, dancing forward a couple of steps and lashing out again. This time, her fist went through the ghost's torso and produced a spray of grayish droplets. The ghost moaned and quivered, then retreated until it was half inside a couple of machines.

"It's working," Craig said, belatedly realizing that he could just point at the ghost.

Following his direction, Tara stepped forward again and jabbed a couple of times, stopping just inches from the machines' windows.

"Hey! What the hell are you doing?"

It was the manager, who'd been somewhere out of sight for a while but was now standing behind her desk. Craig was distracted for a moment. The ghost was less clearly defined when he looked back, and almost totally transparent. In an eyeblink, it shrank to a small, colorless orb that drifted into the street and was soon out of sight.

"It's gone," he gasped.

"Good," Tara said. "Hey, Cappy, are you okay?"

Craig was puzzled until he realized she was talking to the old man. Cappy was not okay. He had slumped sideways in his seat, and his face was pale. A thin trickle of drool appeared at the corner of his open mouth. Craig and Tara almost collided as they ran to help him.

"I'm calling the police!" the manager shouted.

"Make it an ambulance!" Tara yelled. "I think he's having a stroke."

They laid the old man on the seats and his coat to find several layers of clothing. Tara checked for a pulse and described it as good. Not thready, anyway. Cappy's eyes were open, and he seemed to be trying to speak. Craig knelt and listened.

"Go… go before… they get you… no chance… against them…"

Craig kept a lookout for an ambulance or any reappearance of the strange ghost. The manager appeared beside them and took over, and Craig was happy to be ordered around. After they'd gotten the old man comfortable, Tara drew Craig aside.

"The ghost didn't vanish when I hit it?" she asked.

"Not straight away, no," Craig replied.

"Weird. And worrying," she said. "These are not like regular ghosts."

Chief Halloran turned up after about ten minutes. Big patches of sweat under his pits showed that he'd run some distance.

"What happened?" he asked, sounding concerned.

"He had a shock," Craig said. "Something he saw scared him."

The cop gave Craig a quick inscrutable glance before kneeling by the old man.

"Hey Cappy," he said loudly. "You're gonna be okay, old feller, you hear me? Help is on the way."

The reply was just loud enough to be heard over the sound of the laundromat's machines.

"Don't you patronize me, Chuck Halloran. I remember when you were a snot-nosed kid…"

The old man broke off in a fit of coughing that was drowned out by the siren of the ambulance that pulled up a few seconds later. Halloran saw Cappy into the vehicle and then spoke to Craig and Tara, who were standing on the sidewalk. They had not had the opportunity to concoct a story, but Tara had texted Craig.

Keep it simple. No ghosts.

"Now, there's nothing for you folks to be alarmed about," the police chief began. "Old Cappy has had heart trouble for as long as I can remember. Had a hard time in the military. Vietnam generation, you know? He never talks about it. Hell, it's the only thing he won't talk about. We all think he went through the wringer."

"Poor guy," Tara said. "He seemed kind of lonely. Happy to have someone to talk to."

"Yeah, it's a bummer," Halloran agreed. "A war hero but—and I hate to say it—also kind of an outcast. Too argumentative, you see. He's always either rubbing folks the wrong way, or taking offense at nothing, or almost nothing. But we try to take care of him. They'll do tests when they get him to the hospital, and send him back by tonight or tomorrow morning. The point is, don't let this spoil your visit in our lovely town. Normally, we don't get so much drama."

Craig struggled to keep a straight face. Could the guy in charge of law enforcement really not know what haunted the woods?

Maybe that was the point. He knew that some people who underwent trauma emerged able to see the spirits of the dead. If Cappy had come back from Vietnam able to see ghosts and been ridiculed, it would explain a lot. To be mocked could have made the old man clam up and become embittered. Seeing Grendon Mill's abnormal ghosts must have put a tremendous strain on Cappy, especially as he grew older. To be in terror every day but unable to call on anyone for help, to be disbelieved and mocked. It was amazing the poor guy was still alive and reasonably sane.

"Thanks for being so helpful, Inspector," Tara said.

Halloran looked puzzled.

"Sorry, force of habit. I meant Chief," Tara went on. "I lived in

England for a few years, and…"

She faltered, and her pale skin reddened slightly.

And you had a lot of dealings with the cops, Craig thought. *Way to go, partner.*

Halloran's puzzled look vanished at Tara's explanation.

"Oh, is that so? Well, I hope we can offer just as warm a welcome as any little town in England."

The pair seized on this opportunity to shower Grendon Mill with compliments. Halloran left, wishing them well.

"You think he'll check up on us now?" Craig asked.

"If he hasn't already," Tara said. "But that's par for the course, you know? Go into any strange town and ask a lot of questions, the cops might start to sniff around. As a rule, the smaller the town, the more the sniffing. If we do our job right, they'll have nothing concrete to accuse us of, apart from being weird. Which is our constitutional right, last time I checked."

She jerked her head at the entrance to the laundromat.

"Let's go get your nice clean clothes—" she paused, looking at Craig's feet, "and shoes. Then you can tell me all about the ghost I just fought."

CHAPTER 13

COUNCIL OF WAR

They retrieved Craig's clothes and sneakers and then made their way back to the hotel. Craig dropped off his clothes in his room, and they met up, as Tara put it, "to drink coffee and speculate wildly." Tara's hotel room was almost identical to Craig's, except the view was a little better. He could see the town square and the church from the window. His room had a view of the woods.

They sat beside one another on the small couch, Tara with her legs curled up under her, Craig sprawled in semi-exhaustion. Up close, he saw that what he'd taken for a small, rather frail body was muscular and toned. Tara also had a few just-perceptible lines around her eyes and mouth. Even if he hadn't known anything about her, he'd have guessed she'd endured hard times and was now prepared for more.

"What?" she asked after a few minutes of silence.

Craig realized he'd been scrutinizing her.

"Sorry," he said, "but you said you fought against werewolves?"

"Yeah," she replied with no hint of a smile. "Big hairy guys, fangs, love ripping humans apart. Pretty much as advertised."

"Is it true that silver bullets kill them?"

"Among other things," she said. "But silver is effective, yes. Just like iron with ghosts. Hey, I'd love to chat about lycanthropy, but maybe we should focus on our mission?"

The slight awkwardness soon vanished as they went through the day's events. Craig found it easy to talk to Tara. She was patient and intelligent and equipped with a sense of humor. But he was frustrated that he couldn't tell her much about the laundromat ghost that he hadn't already gone through. It might have been the one from the library, but he didn't think so. He had gotten a slightly different vibe. He couldn't be sure whether he'd seen it in the woods, though.

"Minor point, no sweat," Tara remarked at that. "Point is, it was under compulsion from 'The Five', right?"

"'The Five command,'" Craig repeated. "'I have no choice. Pity me.' That's what it said. Or moaned. They moan when they're not shrieking."

"Back in the seventies, the old lumber mill burned down, and five people—maybe four, but let's say five—died."

Craig had already made that connection but felt it was tenuous.

"That could just be a coincidence," he pointed out. "Even if it isn't, are you suggesting that there are five ghosts in charge or something?"

Tara shook her head.

"No. Not yet, at least. Just playing with ideas. We know so little at the moment. But we have some solid facts. The woods are dangerous due to crazy ghosts. Just talking about ghosts is dangerous, as poor old Cappy demonstrated the hard way. It's reasonable to assume that the amulet is in the woods and protected by those ghosts. And the runaways Shane Ryan is looking for ended up in those woods. According to you, at least two of them joined the crazy ghosts. Which reminds me…"

She went to the bedside table to retrieve her phone and jiggled it in front of her.

"I'm going to call him if that's okay with you?"

"Sure," Craig said. "If the guy's as good as his reputation…"

"Quite. And working for collectors is not his M.O., so we're not creating a problem in that respect."

She switched to speaker and dialed the number Shane Ryan had given Craig. The line rang and then there was a terse instruction to leave a message. Tara said she and Craig had located some of the missing youngsters.

"It's not good news, I'm afraid," she added. "Call back, and we'll talk."

She held the phone for a few moments, anticipating a response. When none came, she set it next to her on the bed, and they sipped their coffee for another half-minute.

"Okay. He's either busy or screening his calls," Tara said. "Tell me again about that other ghost. It doesn't fit with the others, and that makes it significant."

Craig went over the description again. Chunky mustache, lurid shirt, mass of curly hair suggesting a perm.

"Let's try and formulate a hypothesis."

"I didn't know we had to have one," he said, baffled. "I mean, I'm sure it's a good thing…"

Tara laughed.

"Just a fancy science word. A hypothesis is when you look at the facts and come up with an explanation that fits them. Then you test it to destruction. That's the scientific method. You try to find data that contradicts the hypothesis. If it survives that test, it might just qualify as a theory."

Craig pondered that.

"So, when some guy on YouTube says he has a theory about what the government's putting into the water supply—"

"He's not using the term correctly, no. He's just cottoned on to an idea that appeals to his prejudices. Not that I'd put anything past the government. But this? Us? We must be rigorous. It's a matter of life and death."

She took out an iPad and brought up a kind of digital whiteboard, then started filling in assorted shapes with data. *Crazy Ghosts. The Five. The Woods. Mustache Guy. Runaways. Amulet. Cappy. Lumber Mill Fire.* It looked like a mess to Craig until he grasped the system. Circles for people and ghosts; rectangles for the rest. Tara connected the various entries. The result was a spiderweb of lines that didn't seem any more enlightening.

"What pisses me off," Tara said, pondering her handiwork, "is that we don't know the amulet's power. I mean, if Stark had just told us it empowers five guys to control ghosts, that would be helpful. I doubt if it's that simple, but any clue would be nice."

"Any point in asking him?" Craig asked.

"I already did before I took the job," she replied. "He said it wasn't relevant. But when I wheedled a little about how it might be dangerous, he said that the thing was inactive."

"Inactive?"

Craig turned the word over in his mind. It sounded like a term you might apply to a bomb or a virus.

"Yeah. Not very reassuring."

"Did you ask him what it looked like?" Craig asked.

"Of course. And I got the distinct impression he hadn't a clue," she said, leaning forward and lowering her voice. "Amazing, right? Mister Know-It-All couldn't tell me. I did a lot of research trying to link an amulet with Grendon Mill or this general area. I got diddly squat."

She paused, looking at Craig closely.

"You know, he staked pretty much everything on your finding it via the local ghosts. He must have had a lot of confidence in you. I was just sent along as backup."

"I'd feel good about that if I hadn't screwed up and nearly gotten killed," Craig moaned.

Tara took a sip of her coffee, winced, and set down the cup.

"Hotel room standard. Still, it's better than in England. I don't think you screwed up, Craig. Not compared to the things I've done. And no, I don't want to talk about them."

She got off the bed and stretched, giving a sigh of relief. Then she began walking up and down the small room, talking while Craig looked on.

"Okay, our hypothesis is this. The Five are linked to the deaths at the old mill in 1976. The ghost you saw today looks like he died around that time. He's our best bet when it comes to finding the amulet, right?"

She stopped pacing to look at Craig, who gave her two thumbs up.

"Okay," Tara continued, pacing again, "so we try to communicate with Mustache Guy next time he pops up."

"Trouble is, he only pops up when there's danger," Craig said gloomily. "So we're down to the crazy ghosts that look weird and are controlled by The Five. And can I add that I really don't want to go into the woods again? Not until we have some means of defending ourselves."

Tara stopped and slapped the flat of her hand against her forehead.

"Ugh, why didn't I think of it before? The woods! We can go into them, but not go into them. Kind of. Let's go."

She grabbed her coat.

"Where are we going?" Craig asked, standing up.

"To my car," she said. "It's time to apply some science."

CHAPTER 14
TRACKS

It was just after five, and the sun was still well clear of the trees. Tara led Craig to her car, explaining what she had planned.

"I got the idea from Marcus," she added. "First time I met him… well, that's irrelevant. Point is, modern tech can help level the playing field when it comes to supernatural threats."

The car, Craig noted, was a new Land Rover Discovery. As they left the hotel parking lot, he commented on what a nice vehicle it was. Tara made a noncommittal noise.

"Expensive to run, not to mention insurance, but I can't do without a vehicle. Lots of stuff to move around. I guess you want to know how much money I'm making at this game?"

Craig started to protest, but she cut him off.

"Come on, money matters to everybody. No need to be embarrassed about it. I'll bet Stark is underpaying you because he can get away with it. Ask for more. A lot more. You put your life on the line today, right?"

"Right," he said.

"I guess driving must be tricky for you?" she asked.

"Too tricky," he agreed. "I was dumb enough to try and learn once. A girlfriend offered to teach me. Said it would transform my life. Turns out, it transformed both our lives. I kept swerving and braking because I couldn't be sure if the person on the road ahead was alive or not. It was one of the things that led to us breaking up."

"Jeez, that's tough. Non-drivers are like second-class citizens in this country."

"Well, I get to walk a lot." Craig tried to sound positive. "I've got very well-defined calf muscles."

"There's always an upside."

They drove out of town and were soon hemmed in by the woods. The road curved slightly, cresting to a low rise, and Craig could no longer see Grendon Mill. They started to discuss their next move, but the conversation was interrupted by the appearance of a police car up ahead. As they drew closer, they saw that Halloran was driving, with another uniformed man in the passenger seat. The police chief raised a hand in salute as they passed. Tara gave a friendly wave.

"Wonder where he's been?" Tara said as soon as the police vehicle was behind them. "No houses out here on the map. No farms, either. Just trees."

"Maybe old Cappy was sent to the big hospital out of town. They could've gone there to take a statement," Craig suggested.

"Two cops for that?" Tara returned. "I doubt it. But let's focus on what we've got to do next. We're nearly there."

A few moments later, they reached a milestone, so badly worn the lettering was almost illegible. Tara pulled over and parked the Discovery.

"You think we're safe parking here?" he asked.

"One thing I found in my research," she said, opening her door, "is that there are no reports of ghosts on the roads leading out of town."

Craig got out, still feeling vulnerable, and asked her why the road would be off-limits.

"After all," he pointed out, "the town is within range of the ghosts."

Tara opened the back of the Discovery and slid a gray metal case onto the tailgate.

"I suspect The Five don't want to draw too much attention," she said, clicking open the catches on the case. "Bus drivers or passengers being terrorized would be too big a story. I bet the runaways killed in the woods never even made it into town."

She opened the lid of the case to reveal the tech she'd talked about earlier. It was a drone, black and spidery, and about two feet across. Craig had seen one like it online.

"A quadcopter, right?"

"Correct," she said, lifting the small machine and handing it to him. "Don't drop it, or it's coming out of your paycheck."

Tara pulled out another case that proved to contain the control system. Craig carefully set the drone on the asphalt and stepped back. Tara flicked a couple of switches and adjusted a small joystick. The drone rose a few inches, then climbed more rapidly until the buzz of its motors faded.

"We have visual," she said.

A screen inside the lid of the case lit up, and Craig saw himself from above, stooping to peer at himself, Tara, and the car. The drone flew off to the left, over the haunted woods. It continued to rise until individual leaves blurred into vague masses of greenery.

"Eye in the sky," he said with wonder. "Do all ghost hunters use this kind of thing?"

"Nah," Tara replied, frowning slightly in concentration. "Not all. But that's because they tend to poke around in old buildings. Not much point in looking at the roof from a hundred feet up."

"Guess not."

Craig moved closer to the screen. The drone passed over trees and more trees. Small clearings showed here and there, but none seemed to contain anything unusual. There were just fallen trees, bright splashes of wildflowers, and delicate shadows cast by saplings. It was almost hypnotic, watching wild nature. Then, it occurred to him that they should have seen a deer or at least a bird by now. Nothing was stirring in the woods.

"No ghosts," Tara muttered. "Guess they're hiding, or they don't register on a digital camera. Does this place look familiar? I'm trying to find the body."

At first, Craig couldn't even begin to guess where he'd been with the fake Tara. But he gave it his best shot, keeping in mind how he had found his way back to the edge of town. He tried to spot signs of a trail made by his chaotic run through the forest, or the more methodical route he'd been forced to take before the ghosts attacked. Neither was apparent.

"Never mind," Tara said. "But you're sure she was attacked in a clearing?"

"Yes," he said. "I—I didn't see her die, though. I just don't think she could've survived."

Tara said nothing but circled the drone for a few more minutes. There was no sign of a corpse. She took the drone higher. This seemed counterintuitive to Craig, and he asked her what she hoped to see.

"I'll know it when I see it," she replied with a quick smile. "Seriously, I want to see the lay of the land. Anything unusual might be a clue."

They saw it after a couple of minutes. A path through the woods, just barely perceptible, and invisible at lower altitudes. At first, Craig thought it was the route he and the impostor had taken. But then Tara swept the drone around and followed the trail back to the road. Soon, the Land Rover came into view again. The beaten track began at the milestone.

"Somebody parked here and walked into the woods along that route quite a few times," Tara said. "Let's see where it leads. I think that's a small clearing?"

The drone started to descend, and Craig saw a vaguely rectangular shape at the end of the track. Before it came into clearer focus, he was startled by a burst of sound from a police siren. Chief Halloran's cruiser was back, pulling up in front of the Discovery.

"Damn," Tara cursed under her breath. "Try and buy a little time, huh?"

Craig dutifully walked over to the police car as Halloran and the other officer got out. He felt self-conscious asking, 'Is there a problem, Officer?' as it was such a massive cliché, but it was also the only obvious thing to say.

Halloran was his usual friendly self.

"No problem, Craig, just a friendly word of advice. Best not to stay parked here. It's technically illegal, unless you got engine trouble?"

"No, no, we were just flying a drone to… to look at the scenery, get some footage."

"My fault," Tara called. "I love filming every place I go from all angles. I'm bringing it in now."

"Sorry to spoil your fun," the chief went on, ambling a little closer, "but I can't go making exceptions. If I were you, I'd fly your thingamajig over the river. Some lovely views up the valley."

"We'll certainly do that," Craig said as the drone appeared, a black dot growing rapidly larger.

"Well, we'll be moving along," Halloran said. "See you folks around town, no doubt."

"No doubt," Tara called cheerily.

Far from moving on, the cops sat in their car and watched until the outsiders packed up the drone. Only then did Halloran execute a three-point turn and head back into town.

"Well, we still learned something," Tara said as they climbed into the Discovery.

"Two things," Craig pointed out.

As he'd hoped, Tara looked uncomprehending.

"You didn't notice their shoes?" he asked. "Just like mine were, covered in mulch and leaves. Like they recently trekked through the forest along that path you found. Maybe that's where they've been?"

CHAPTER 15

WALK AND TALK

"You think they took the body?" Tara asked as they drove back into town.

"Yeah," he said. "Halloran is in on it. Must be. Why would he be out roaming the woods with his deputy, or whoever that was?"

Tara had to agree but had a caveat.

"Why didn't they just bury that woman in the woods? Seems like an ideal place."

"Takes time, I guess," Craig said. "I've never buried a body, but I always think the movies make it look too easy."

"Yeah, I guess," Tara said.

They discussed their next move. So far, Shane Ryan had not responded to Tara's messages. They were on their own, and it seemed that the mysterious Five included Halloran and maybe his as-yet-nameless deputy. Other candidates were the librarian and the minister.

"Not sure about them, though," Craig said. "Librarians generally don't like people making a fuss, which I certainly did. So maybe it's just that. As for the minister—well, he was friendly enough. Maybe he doesn't believe in ghosts and has convinced himself everything is hunky-dory. I've found that people have a huge capacity for self-deception."

"But he's an authority figure in a small town," Tara pointed out. "If this Five outfit controls things, it would be surprising if they were just five nobodies."

Something about this argument bothered Craig. It related to the way Stark dressed like he'd just raided a thrift store. But he was unsure of himself yet again and said nothing. Instead, he stared ahead as the hotel came into view, a mishmash of ideas vying for his attention as Tara spoke again.

"And besides, can you really take seriously a supposed man of God who doesn't think there's anything strange going on in this town?"

"None so blind as those who will not see," Craig said. "Maybe he doesn't want to face the truth?"

There were only three other cars parked outside the hotel, the spring season still getting underway. They pulled up alongside a newcomer, a battered station wagon crammed with fishing gear.

"Genuine visitors or amulet hunters?" Tara said as they got out. "If they're on the hunt, their cover is pretty good."

Craig looked inside the station wagon. There was a baseball cap on the passenger seat, but it didn't bear any of the usual logos. Instead, it was decorated with a picture of two round fishing floats, under which was the phrase "Show Us Your Bobbers". He pointed this out to his partner.

"Tasteful," Tara said. "I think these guys are the real deal. Okay, shall we walk into town? It's about time we ate dinner, in my humble opinion. Oh, but before we do that, something I forgot earlier. It won't take a minute. Wait for me in the lobby."

Craig sat flicking through tourist brochures for considerably more than a minute. The desk clerk smiled benignly at him. The young woman seemed genuine, but who could tell? He knew he was growing paranoid, as most residents of Grendon Mill must be what they seemed.

A little too much so, he thought.

Tara reappeared with a backpack and led him back to the car. Once inside, she took out a few items. A Taser, "useless against ghosts but effective against humans who might control ghosts," according to her. She also offered him a set of iron knuckledusters.

"These ghosts don't disappear when you hit them with iron, but they still seem to flinch. Or would you prefer an iron dagger?" Tara suggested. "You can see them, after all. I'd hate to have to fight a bunch of them."

Craig hesitated. He didn't want to be seen as unprofessional or a big wuss. But attacking ghosts in any way went against the grain.

"You don't think of yourself as a fighter?" Tara said with a trace of disappointment. "But Craig, you'll have to be a fighter in this game. People—and a lot of things that aren't people—won't just hand over the goods."

"I know," he said, resentful at how right she was.

He took the knuckledusters. Tara rummaged some more and produced a dull metal disk on a cord. A pendant. She held it up, showing Craig that it bore unfamiliar symbols.

"Marcus told me about this," she said. "It's some kind of Norse charm, a *vegvisir*. I got this one from a guy called James Moran. You heard of him?"

Craig hadn't. He turned the pendant over. It was made of iron and decorated with odd symbols.

"Runic letters," Tara explained. "The *vegvisir* is the 'shower of the way', or so the story goes. It helps you find your way home through any storm or darkness. I carry one all the time."

"Does it work?" Craig asked dubiously.

"No idea. I've been lucky enough not to get lost, but if Marcus says it's useful…"

Craig was getting a little tired of hearing about the amazing Marcus Mortlake, the eccentric British professor who seemed to know everything. But Tara held the guy in high esteem, presumably with good reason. He put on the pendant, tucking the iron disc down inside his shirt. It was cold against his skin.

"Guess it's better to have it and not need it," he said, "than to need it and not have it."

"That's the right attitude," Tara grinned. "Now, shall we take a stroll to the diner and see what their evening menu has to offer the discerning connoisseur?"

They talked as they walked, going over what they knew and what they didn't. The latter was a much bigger category, but Tara seemed quite perky at the thought of further confrontations.

"I don't do this because it's relaxing," she said when he pointed this out. "I went through some things when I first realized I had a wild talent. Hell, I'm still working on it, trying to build a new life. I wanted to run away at first, hide in my science career, pretend the paranormal didn't exist."

Craig felt a wave of empathy for her.

"I felt the same when I was a kid. I didn't want to be different. Everyone thinks if you have a special power, it's like what you see in the movies, but it's the opposite. You can't live a normal life. I told people I saw ghosts a few times, but all that got me was trouble. I was nearly locked away in a psychiatric clinic…"

"Guess I'm lucky, nobody ever tried to section me—but I see what you mean," Tara said. "You know, the only superhero that's realistic is the Hulk. The original Hulk, when he couldn't control it. Because my power is linked to my emotions, and that takes a lot of mental discipline to make it work and not hurt innocent people."

Her upbeat manner was gone for a moment, but then it returned, like a small cloud briefly obscuring the sun.

"Hey, tell me more about Craig Ellison," she said. "It can't have just been terrible driving lessons and ghosts."

"There's not much to tell," he replied, looking down at the sidewalk. "I see ghosts, it gave me a lot of problems, I took a series of dead-end, minimum-wage jobs. I eventually washed up in an obscure town and found a pub where I could sit and drink and not be bothered by ghosts. That was where I met Stark."

Tara mulled that over for a while.

"Yeah, this pub—Hannigan's, right? That place must have some serious defenses. Paranormal entities hate being barred from any place in the mortal realm. Who runs it?"

"A guy called Harry. Vietnam vet, I think."

"So he's an old guy," Tara mused. "I guess that scans if he's an adept of some kind. Takes decades to develop that level of power."

It took Craig a few moments to grasp her meaning. Then he laughed.

"Harry as some kind of magician? He's a bartender. He grumbles about having to do the monthly accounts."

Tara shrugged.

"Okay, so who owns the place? Is there a Mr. Hannigan?"

Craig thought back to the times he had heard Harry and the other staff talk about the pub's owner in hushed tones. Not exactly fear, but a kind of awe. And not one of the customers Craig talked to had ever seen the guy. He told Tara this.

"Right, so there's a guy nobody has seen who owns a pub with perfect psychic barriers against ghosts and demons and whatnot. And Stark sits in this guy's bar dishing out weird quests to people like you and me. Think there might be a connection?"

It was Craig's turn to shrug.

"I guess, but there's no point in asking Stark…"

He stopped walking and stared at her.

"Hey, do you think Stark works for Mr. Hannigan? That he's the mysterious collector?"

Tara raised a well-defined eyebrow. They walked on to the diner, discussing possibilities.

CHAPTER 16

NIGHTFALL

Dinner at the diner was uneventful. The meal was good, the place was busy, and nobody acted strangely. Craig and Tara were treated like regular tourists. If word had gotten around about Cappy's mishap, it wasn't being seen as their fault.

They were both a little exhausted and not much inclined to talk. They just ate wholesome food, drank decent coffee, and stared out the window. Craig half-expected to see either a crazy ghost or Mustache Guy, but neither appeared. He saw the police cruiser pass by, moving slowly. Chief Halloran looked back at Craig, his eyes shielded by sunglasses. The cop did not acknowledge Craig in any way.

"What gives?" Tara asked.

She'd been busy with a rare steak.

"Halloran," Craig explained. "Checking up on us, maybe."

"Well, we are law-abiding citizens," she said, "so, sucks to him."

Craig watched her eating, holding her knife in her right hand, and pointing the tines of her fork downward. It was the British way of using cutlery. He recalled seeing it on TV shows. He commented on it, and she laughed.

"I started doing it subconsciously, I guess, and the habit just stuck. I daresay I'll switch back to a more free and easy approach in time."

"Do you miss living in England?" he asked.

Tara took a mouthful of steak and thought it over.

"I miss some things. I made friends and had some fun despite… all the bad stuff. But I guess I'll always see it as the place where I learned too much too soon. Too much about myself. And the way the world really is."

Craig understood that. He felt the same way about his hometown. He dreaded going back there but was also racked with guilt every time he called his folks and explained why he couldn't make it for Christmas or Thanksgiving yet again.

They strolled around town after the meal and Tara took a look at the church. The lack of Grendon tombstones came up again. Craig wondered if there might be some link to The Five. It seemed odd that a go-getting lumber baron should found a town, only to have his dynasty die out after a couple of generations.

"You think The Five took over and wiped out the Grendons?" Tara mulled it over. "Guess that might be the case. But bear in mind that surnames pass through the male line. One generation consisting solely of married daughters can extinguish a name. For all we know, old man Grendon's descendants are all around us."

At her suggestion, they walked to the riverbank and went a quarter mile or so upstream. They found a small, pleasant park where a few people walked dogs or were just out for an evening stroll.

"They created the park after the lumber mill burned down," Tara said. "Nothing left of it now, but it stood somewhere around here."

A small bandstand stood in the middle of the park, and they ambled over to it and sat on a bench under the canopy. Craig hoped that some regular ghosts might be present. People who died in a fire often lingered on the earthly plane. Those whose lives were unexpectedly cut short made classic ghosts.

"Anything?" Tara asked after they'd been sitting silently for a few minutes.

"No," Craig said. "At least, nothing definite. But I am getting a sense of something unusual…"

An image flashed into his mind, blotting out the pleasant view of the park. He got an impression of darkness, robed figures, candles placed at the points of a black pentagram within a circle, and shapes marked on bare boards. He glimpsed machinery in the shadows—the gleam of metal. Craig was looking down onto the group, maybe from a gantry or balcony about twenty feet above floor level.

The vision disappeared, and he gasped in shock.

"What is it?"

Tara was reaching into her coat pocket, presumably for a weapon. Craig held up a hand to reassure her. After a few heartbeats, he found his voice.

"Not a ghost, or at least not in the usual sense. I saw something. I've never had a vision before, but I think that was one. I saw a ritual being performed. It was in the mill, I guess. Before the fire."

He described what he'd seen as best he could.

"Impressive," Tara said. "You saw The Five. And they seem to be the usual bunch of demon-worshipping jerks—pentagrams, robes, candles. Seen their sort so many times. Normally, they don't achieve much, just get off on being part of a supposed elite group. Except…"

She looked out toward the riverbank. Craig, following her gaze, saw nothing but a man trying to fly a kite for his small son while a woolly-coated dog ran around and barked in excitement.

"Except that a bunch of jerks couldn't have created those weird ghosts?" he suggested.

"Yeah, those weirdos prove we're up against some dangerous power," she agreed. "The Five might have been a bunch of sophomores playing at Satanism, but they must have genuine power. And it's been passed down somehow, by offspring or recruitment. One of them must have survived that fire to form a new group. If they indeed died in the fire."

"What I don't get," Craig said, "is whose viewpoint I saw the ritual from. Somebody on a walkway above the main floor of the old lumber mill. I got the feeling it was all a bit sneaky."

"An interloper, I guess," Tara said. "Someone spying on them, maybe trying to expose their antics."

They talked some more as the evening wore on. They set off back to the hotel as night began to fall. Tara tried to contact Shane Ryan. Again, there was no answer.

"Guess he takes being a loner very seriously," Craig remarked.

"Hmm," Tara said. "We'll just have to soldier on. Do you think if you went to sleep in that pavilion, you'd dream some more about The Five?"

Craig smiled. The park gates would close in a few minutes.

"Are you suggesting we climb over the fence in the middle of the night?"

"Why not?" she shot back. "But okay, it might lead to awkward questions. Maybe we can come up with a better idea if we sleep on it. Marcus often had prophetic dreams in his sleep. Maybe that's a talent you could cultivate?"

Craig almost said he'd heard enough about the wonderful Marcus but stopped himself in time.

"I talk about him a lot, don't I?" Tara said more quietly. "But he convinced me I wasn't crazy, that the world isn't always rational and scientific. And that was hard to accept. Marcus helped me a lot to come to terms with it."

"Did you have—you know, adventures?" Craig asked. "Solving mysteries, stuff like that?"

He expected her to laugh, but Tara didn't look up at him.

"I killed his vampire girlfriend. And I killed some guys when I was possessed. Not what I'd call adventures."

Craig wanted to ask a lot more questions but knew it would be tactless. Instead, he tried desperately to think of another topic. When they got back to the hotel, he was still trying.

CHAPTER 17
VISITATION

For the first time in a while, Craig had no ghosts to wish him goodnight.

He closed the curtains to blot out the woods, which were still just visible against the glow of twilight. Then he got undressed, showered, brushed his teeth, and realized he'd forgotten to bring anything to sleep in. He improvised with a sweatshirt and boxers and slid under the covers.

Sleep did not come easily. He slumbered for a short while, woke, checked the time, then tried to drop off again. He recalled his mother saying that the Sandman is sometimes downright negligent in his duties. That had been when he was five and the sobbing ghost of a murder victim had upset him so much that he had not slept for a week.

In this instance, Craig blamed the traumas of the day, the strange bed, and the general air of displacement. For all that, he blamed Stark, which was only reasonable. The guy had blundered by not giving each of his agents a picture of the other. Every time Craig closed his eyes, he saw the distorted forms of the ghosts attacking the woman who wasn't Tara. He didn't even know her name. That she was a nameless victim somehow seemed to make it worse. Sure, she was one of the bad guys. She might well have shot him and left him to bleed out in the woods if they'd found the amulet.

Still, he thought, *a life is a life. If I don't care about her at all, I'm as bad as she was.*

Craig tried to steer his mind onto happier subjects, but it seemed his train of thought was constantly switched to bleaker destinations. He recalled one occasion when he'd seen a psychiatrist, at his parents' insistence. Craig had been seventeen. The woman was kind, intelligent, and unwilling to accept the existence of ghosts. She had explained that little Craig had invented his ability to make himself feel special, and adolescent Craig had just clung on to that childish fantasy.

"But I don't want to feel special," he'd protested. "It's not like I'm having adventures with an invisible friend or something. I hate seeing the dead."

"You tell yourself you hate it, but it gets attention, which makes you feel special," the shrink had replied. "We have to find out why your mind conjured up this particular fantasy."

It was during one of those frustrating sessions that Craig admitted to harboring thoughts of joining the dead because there was no way he could beat them. They would always be there, denying him a normal life. If he killed himself, he'd explained, he would no longer be harassed by the unquiet dead. The angry ones, the sad ones, the lonely ones—they only talked to him because he was alive.

The psychiatrist had been compassionate, even helpful.

"Craig," she had said, "when someone does what you are contemplating, a whole world is destroyed. A world still in the making. A world that is, yes, bleak and terrible in some ways. But also, a world that holds joys and wonders unimagined. Every human being is a little cosmos, a kind of pocket universe if you like. I'd urge you to reconsider."

Craig wasn't very impressed with that argument, so she'd given him some more practical information. Like how many people ended up terribly injured by suicide attempts. How often she had seen the horrible impact on loved ones. "If you love anyone at all, do you want to hurt them so badly?" That combination of inspiring sermon and guilt trip had worked.

The oddest thing was, as Craig lay in the hotel bed with his eyes firmly shut, he could not recall that doctor's name. It quickly became an obsession, a rabbit hole down which he raced, running through possible combinations. Was it Doctor Barker? Something like that. Barkiss?

Bradlaugh? It began with a B, he felt sure. Or was it Carlton?

"It's Gates."

No way, he thought. *Definitely not Gates.*

Then, Craig froze. The voice had not been in his head. Someone had spoken the word, close by, in the darkness.

Craig lay very still, heart pounding, listening for the sound of movement. There was none. He opened his eyes and slowly turned his head. A faint glow illuminated the small couch that sat under the window. A nebulous blur of colorless light gradually increased and took on definition. Details emerged. A chunky mustache, boots with Cuban heels, and flared pants.

Mustache Guy. Craig sat up and almost shouted.

"Who are you?"

"I just told you, Gates. Alva Gates."

The ghost got up and walked over to the bed. Gates stood expressionless as Craig scrambled out from under the covers. He was exhilarated but also scared. It was great to encounter a normal ghost, the kind he'd spent his adult life speaking to and trying to help. But so far, Gates had been a harbinger of doom, appearing when the crazy ghosts were nearby.

"Am I in danger?" he asked, pulling on his jeans.

"We're all in danger," Gates said.

His voice was rich and resonant, as if he was accustomed to public speaking. Or maybe he was an actor? It certainly reinforced Craig's sense of the guy having escaped from an old TV show. Maybe Rockford or the original Hawaii Five-O. He had watched reruns of such shows when he'd stayed with his grandparents.

"Yes," Craig insisted, fumbling with his zipper in the dark, "but I mean specifically me and now. The crazy ghosts, are they coming?"

Gates' eyes widened and he looked around in alarm. His form shimmered slightly, losing its clear outline.

"Are they coming? How do you know?"

"I don't, jeez," Craig responded. "It's just… you warned me before. That's not why you're here now?"

Gates relaxed, his form reverting to its realistic appearance.

"No," he said. *"I'm here to tell you what you need to know. Only I don't know how long I have. My enemies are always working against me. Their powers grow stronger by the day."*

Craig introduced himself and then asked the obvious question.

"Who are The Five?"

Gates shook his head.

"I do not know. They mask themselves both literally and with occult power. Most times, they are ordinary people. And as individuals, they are nothing. Only when they band together can they control the disembodied."

The word puzzled Craig. It was an odd term for ghosts. He was about to ask why Gates used it when the ghost emitted a moan of pain, or terror, or both. Gates clutched his head, bent forward, and gasped.

"The Five. They are assembled somewhere nearby. They're reaching out to try and strike at me. But I can evade them…"

Gates straightened up and held out his arms straight at his sides. Then he began to recite something in a low voice, eyes shut, concentrating intensely. The room grew cold, and Craig shuddered. Flecks of blackness, like soot whirling in the air, clustered around Gates. They began to accumulate into a shape, like a poor charcoal sketch of a skeleton. The thing shrieked and writhed. An oval-shaped face appeared, with three black blurs marking the huge eyes and open mouth.

Craig climbed back onto the bed, retreating headlong. Then he remembered the knuckledusters Tara had given him. They were in his coat pocket. The coat he'd casually flung onto the couch earlier. He had nothing to use as a weapon. The crazy ghost moved toward him, passing into the bed. Its fingers reached out, long black twigs that he knew would pierce and rend his soul. He backed off some more and collided with the wall.

"Help!" he yelled pointlessly.

The deranged ghost closed in. Then it stopped, flickered, and seemed to collapse in on itself. It vanished in a burst of black shards that faded into the shadows. Behind it, the ghost of Alva Gates was on his knees, eyes still shut tight, arms raised, still chanting under his breath.

"Was that—did you do that?" Craig asked.

The ghost stopped chanting and looked at him. Gates smiled for the first time, revealing dazzling teeth, one of which was gold.

"Yeah. Reckon I still got it."

"Thank you," Craig said, collapsing onto the bed to sit opposite Gates. "How did you do that?"

The ghost shrugged.

"Willpower, knowledge, innate talent—in about equal portions. You got all three, you're cooking with gas. Lack one of them, though, and you're as good as dead."

Craig didn't know what to say. Gates saved him the trouble, laughing loudly at himself. Or at Craig's expression. Or maybe a bit of both.

"Yeah, I know, heavy irony because I'm dead meat myself. Have been for a while now. But those were special circumstances. Five against one, those are lousy odds. Plus, I wasn't really ready that time."

Craig found himself warming to the ghost. Gates' voice was still resonant like he was speaking to an audience of more than one.

"So… what happened?" he asked eagerly.

Gates didn't reply. He was looking past Craig, head cocked to one side, as though straining to listen.

"They'll attack again," he said after a few seconds. *"I've got to go. You're in danger. That poor creature you just saw was after me, not you, but it was confused. They always are. I need to get the facts across to you somehow…"*

Gates took a step toward Craig and then hesitated. Seen up close, the ghost's face was not quite so lifelike. It seemed to be a kind of patchwork of irregular pieces of flesh. Then Craig realized that he was seeing scars, a pattern of horrific injuries that crisscrossed Gates' features. He gasped.

"What happened to your face?"

"You really are a top-grade seer," the ghost said, his voice sad and reflective. *"What you see are the injuries of many dead innocents. But it's too complicated to explain… I have to go now, but I'll be back. Count on it."*

CHAPTER 18
THAT SEVENTIES GUY

"Wait!" Craig cried.

Gates was already starting to fade, the light he radiated once more colorless, his form ill-defined, and then a mere hazy orb that shrank to a dot and vanished. Sitting in the dark once more, Craig grabbed his phone and called Tara. It took half a minute for her to respond, but once he'd gotten through the gist of the encounter, she was all business.

"Stay put. I'll be right there."

After the call ended, Craig remembered the iron knuckledusters and put them on. After a few moments of contemplating the weapon, he shifted it from his right hand to his left. He might need to use his phone again.

It seemed like a long wait, but she arrived within five minutes, barefoot and wrapped in a coat that just about concealed an oversized T-shirt. She threw a bag onto the couch. It landed heavily, and Craig heard metal clinking.

"Tools of the trade, remember," she said. "Now, what the hell happened…"

Tara trailed off and Craig realized she was looking down at his feet. More precisely, at his right foot. The flesh where his little toe had been severed was still bright red. It had only been a couple of months since the incident.

"Russian mob," he said. "Took it off with bolt cutters."

"Oh God, I'm sorry, staring like that," Tara said, sitting on the couch. "Don't tell me, Stark got you into that situation?"

"Yeah. I'll put some socks on."

Embarrassed for both of them, he rummaged in his bag for socks and dragged them on. He talked nervously as he did so, describing Alva Gates and trying to sum up what had happened. Tara listened carefully while taking various items out of her bag. She laid two iron daggers on the armrests of the couch and placed a Taser in her lap. Then she produced a BB pistol.

"Iron pellets," she explained, holding it out to him. "Engages the enemy at long range. Well, longer than arms' length, anyway."

He took the black pistol and weighed it in his free hand. He'd shot BB guns as a kid but not since. He took an experimental shot into the pillow. The pellet made a satisfying thud. He laid the pistol within reach on the nightstand and sat down again.

"So, Alva Gates," Tara said, taking out her phone. "Let's see if the crummy internet here holds up… there we go. And with a name like Alva… here he is."

She got up and sat next to Craig, showing him a page of hits. All were from websites dealing with the paranormal. Tara's first try was a dead link. The website had been defunct for years.

"Not promising," she remarked. "But we soldier on."

The next link was to a site concerning mysterious disappearances. It referred only in passing to Gates as having gone missing in the autumn of 1976. But there was very little information about the man. He had achieved some fame for his supposed psychic powers, which had been tested by a professor of physics at Harvard. This level of academic interest surprised Craig.

"Not so strange for the seventies," Tara said. "There was a brief period from World War II through about 1980—when reputable and semi-reputable researchers looked into ESP. Spent a small fortune in some cases. You must have seen those Zener cards—you know, like in Ghostbusters? The cards with circles, waves, stars, and the like?"

"Yeah, I remember that scene," Craig said. "But why was there so much interest?"

"Cold War anxiety played a part. If the Russians had telepaths, Uncle Sam had to have 'em too. Some of the scientists were straight-up working for the CIA, NSA, or the military. Others were more interested in pure knowledge. But it all died out by the late eighties. A bit like disco and pet rocks."

"So, what happened?" Craig asked. "I mean, why didn't the scientists keep doing tests and stuff?"

"That… is… a very… good… question," Tara said, not looking up as she scrolled and clicked, rejected a site, and went back to find another. "Aha. Here we are."

There was a brief biography of Gates on a clunky, lurid site devoted to Mysterious Powers of the Mind. He was born in Salt Lake City in 1934, served in Vietnam, and when he returned home, he drifted from job to job. He'd gained a reputation for his mindreading abilities in the early seventies. He had a gig in Vegas as the Amazing Alva and earned good money.

"He was seen as a rival to Kreskin and Uri Geller," Tara said. "The big-time beckoned and… oh my God."

Craig had to laugh. The picture that accompanied the story was of Gates on stage. He was dressed in a way that, as Tara remarked, made Elvis Presley's Vegas outfits look quite restrained. It seemed the man had a taste for bright clothing and spiral perms. He was grinning cheesily at the camera. A gold medallion was nestled in abundant chest hair. A couple of showgirls in skimpy sequined leotards and pink-plumed headgear posed on either side. Behind the striking threesome was an arch bearing the words "The Amazing Alva".

"Well, he saw his name in lights," Craig said.

"They call it the decade that taste forgot," Tara observed. "Can't see why."

"He gave all that up and died here, and nobody knew." Craig was sobered by the thought. "Why? What was so serious that he threw away money and fame?"

"Threw away incipient fame," Tara pointed out. "His career pretty much crashed on takeoff. That's why we never heard of the guy. He was a great might-have-been."

She found a newspaper article that mentioned the Harvard research, but further clicks drew a blank. Website after website rehashed the same information and picture. The only other image was a grainy photo probably scanned from an old news item. It showed Gates looking almost unrecognizable, in uniform with short hair, his expression serious. A young man going off to war. A picture from some regiment's archive, perhaps. The photo was cropped from a larger one. Next to Gates, the right shoulder and part of the face of another man were visible.

"Ironic," Craig said. "Going off to war, surviving, then dying fighting some terrible evil in your own country."

"Why him, though?" Tara asked quietly, staring at the picture. "Why did Alva Gates, of all people, come to confront The Five? What brought him here?"

Craig felt parts of a puzzle slotting into place. He could almost hear the clicks in his head.

"Cappy," he said. "He's a Vietnam vet. With paranormal ability. It's too much of a coincidence."

Tara raised her hand for a high-five, which Craig was happy to take part in. He felt they were meshing better as a team now that they'd started solving problems. More importantly, he was contributing and not just tagging along.

"Okay, Cappy is our go to guy," Tara said. "First thing tomorrow, we try to get him to talk."

"Sounds like a plan," said Alva Gates, leaning between them.

"Oh my God!" Craig yelled, leaping to his feet.

Tara stood up and grabbed a dagger from the couch before facing the bed, aiming at nothing in particular.

"Is it another one?"

"It's only Gates, it's fine. Just nearly gave me a heart attack, is all," Craig said. And to Gates, he added, "Alva, this is Tara. She's—"

Gates, who had been standing in the middle of the bed, raised his hands in an apologetic gesture.

"Hey, sorry fella. Guess the little lady can't see me? Pity, she's quite the babe. And we all know about redheads, right?"

Craig laughed nervously.

"What is it?" Tara asked, still pointing the dagger.

"He's just sorry he startled me—us," Craig said. "And he's back at the ideal moment. Now Alva can tell us about his connection to Cappy."

Craig looked expectantly at Gates as Tara lowered the iron blade. The ghost looked from one person to the other, his expression puzzled.

"I'll help in any way I can," Gates said, *"but who the hell is Cappy?"*

CHAPTER 19
THE AMAZING ALVA

The conversation that ensued was difficult. Tara couldn't see or hear Gates, so Craig had to act as a translator. Tara asked a question that Gates could hear and Craig relayed the ghost's reply. That was the least of their problems because as they talked some more, it became clear that Gates' memory was impaired. In fact, it was a train wreck of fragmentary facts and impressions. He was also prone to wander off on tangents.

"What happened to my car?" he kept asking.

The car in question was—or had been—a '75 Dodge Challenger with Morocco leather upholstery. For some reason, Gates kept fretting about Zelda, as he called the car. Craig did his best to get the ghost back onto more relevant topics. It wasn't easy.

"He's been through the wringer," Craig explained to Tara. "It's left him in a bad way."

"Why are you in a bad way?" she asked, staring at a point a few inches above Gates' head.

"Why?" the ghost said. *"The Five, that's why. Those bastards have been gunning for me since I got here. They've come so close to breaking me many times. Left me in a hell of a… oh my God, just talking about it… I think… oh Jesus, not again."*

The ghost swayed and faded slightly before becoming opaque again. Once more, Craig saw Gates' face become a network of reddish-black fissures. This time, the impression did not fade. Instead, it became worse. Gates' left eye was suddenly a gaping concavity half-filled with rotten flesh and dried blood. His nose was slit up the middle. He wailed in pain to reveal a mouth almost devoid of teeth. Bloody stumps oozed.

"Oh my God," Craig gasped.

"What is it?" Tara asked, alarmed.

"He's been tortured. They did horrible things to him before he died. I've seen something like this before, but never this bad."

Gates' body was now covered in wounds. His garish clothes became shreds of torn nylon or vanished completely. He was nearly naked, and his body was a mass of bruises and gaping wounds. Craig didn't look away, feeling this would somehow dishonor the dead man. Gates doubled over, still wailing, until he was curled on the floor in a fetal position.

"Not before…"

The words were barely audible.

"Not before?" Craig repeated, crouching by the whimpering ghost.

"After. After I died. They killed me… then tortured me," Gates rasped. *"Over and over. So many times. But I never told them. Never gave it back."*

"Gave what back?" Craig asked, gesturing at Tara for quiet. "Do you mean the amulet?"

The only reply was a terrible howl, more like a wounded beast than a human being. Alva Gates' body spasmed and writhed. Then he flung out his limbs and lay splayed out on the floor. The torture-wracked body began to rot, the few remnants of undamaged flesh blackening and falling away to reveal broken bones. Gates' remaining eye clouded and collapsed into a mass of putrefaction.

Craig described it to Tara, who listened pale-faced but still put a reassuring hand on his shoulder.

"It's over," he said flatly when Gates' bones were all that remained.

And then, the whole process began again. The phantom form of the long-dead man reformed out of thin air, Gates' mouth wide in a scream of suffering. It took Craig a few moments to grasp that this time, the process was faster: the phases of injury, death, and decay speeding by.

And then it began a third time and a fourth. What had taken minutes was now happening in a dozen heartbeats. All the while, Alva Gates moaned, howled, and yelled in agony, only for his voice to finally fail in a gurgling or retching as death claimed him once more.

"Oh my God," Craig whispered.

"What?" demanded Tara. "Talk to me, Craig."

"He died. More than once."

"I don't understand," she said, hunkering down beside him. "What do you mean? Was it reincarnation?"

"I have no idea how it happened," Craig said, turning from the horrific sight to look into her eyes. "I just know that, somehow, he was tortured to death again and again. I don't know how. Can The Five bring you back to life? Resurrect the body?"

"Not a living body," Tara said skeptically. "The undead exist, and they're tough bastards. It takes a lot to put them down. But from what you've described, this is something new. Well, new to me…"

Craig looked back down at Gates. The cycle was reaching its end once more, a twisted skeleton all that remained of the victim. Then the form of a living man, with flesh and garish clothing intact, began to form once again.

"I think," Craig said, "we're going to have to be patient with Alva."

Craig lost count of the number of times Gates was tortured to death in front of him, but the terrible process finally ended after at least ten cycles. Gates lay for a moment, staring up at the ceiling. Then he sat up and stared at Craig.

"My friend, you have serious power. You saw right through my whole timeline there. All the way back to the start. Back to the start of it all. My demise, my terrible demise…"

The ghost trailed off as Craig stared at him.

"I don't have that ability," Craig protested. "I've never been able to…"

He hesitated. He'd never encountered a ghost like Gates. Add to that the way Gates had died multiple times, and Craig was way out of his depth.

Then throw in the power of the amulet, and all bets were off.

"Yeah, well, you see it now," Gates said, standing up. *"A ghost seer that's strong enough affects the ghost he's observing. Some kind of physics involved, maybe. I don't know. Maybe our little science babe would know."*

Craig conveyed the gist of Gates' thoughts to Tara.

"Wow," was her reaction. "Yeah, it's true when you're measuring the properties of an electron or whatever that the observer has an effect. If you accurately measure the velocity, you can get the location exactly right."

"Smart cookie," Gates said. *"Brains and beauty, I always liked that—it's a helluva sexy combination. Not all men like brainy women, of course. But then, I guess I'm a feminist."*

Craig turned a burst of laughter into a coughing fit. Tara was too absorbed in thought to notice.

"Hell, maybe ghosts are like quantum particles. It would explain them being able to walk through walls and stuff. And maybe iron or other ferrous metals somehow disrupt their magnetic properties…"

She shook her head, making a dismissive gesture.

"No, that's irrelevant. Can't you just tell us where the amulet is?"

Craig looked expectantly at Gates.

The ghost smiled and raised his right hand, his fingers tightly clenched.

"Right here. I kept hold of it right to the end."

Gates opened his fist to reveal not an amulet but a red indentation in his flesh where something had been held tight in his dying moments. There was a trace of some kind of chain or lanyard wrapped around a diamond-shaped object about two inches by one.

Craig told Tara that the amulet was with Gates' body and described its outline.

"And that body is where?" Tara asked.

"Oh, I can take you there right now if you like," Gates said. *"I died in the woods."*

CHAPTER 20

THE MELDING

"He says it's in the woods," Craig explained to Tara. "His body."

"But we'll get killed if we go into the woods," Tara said, staring at Gates' right shoulder. "You know that, right?"

Gates chuckled.

"Oh yeah, I keep forgetting. Sorry, my mind's a little scrambled. Okay, let me focus. First, you gotta get past the discarnates. Now, that's tricky…"

Craig seized upon the word.

"The discarnates—those weird ghosts, right? Why are they like that?"

Gates held up his hands in mock appeal.

"Hey, hey fella, that's a lot of questions, and I… I…"

The ghost's expression changed to show distress, and his mouth twisted in pain. His form grew hazy, blurring and losing color until a vaguely man-shaped cloud of mist stood in the room. Then Gates phased back in, becoming solid once more.

Seeing Craig's expression, Tara asked, "What's going on? What's he saying?"

"Crap, that was difficult," the ghost said. *"They keep trying to get to me. They keep interfering."*

"The Five? Are they on your trail?" Craig asked.

Gates nodded.

"Bastards. I came here to stop them, the first Five that is, and I did. But… oh… look… this is too hard. I just have to think about them, and they sense it. Waves of energy go out, they feel my thoughts, and my pain, like spiders sensing movement in their webs…"

Gates leaned closer to Craig.

"You need to know a lot because they're planning another ritual. I can feel it like a gathering storm. There'll be another killing. Soon. It'll be soon."

"How soon?" Tara asked after Craig passed on the info.

"A day, maybe two at most," Gates said. *"The sacrifice has to be during the hour that belongs to the dead. Midnight to one AM. There are other factors at work, but that's the main rule. I still wish I knew what they'd done with my goddamn car…"*

Craig relayed this to Tara, who pointed out that it was already well after two and yawned for emphasis. Craig, too, was tired. Despite the weird circumstances, his eyelids were drooping. But he recalled what Gates had said when he first appeared. He and Tara were in danger.

"Will there be more attacks on us tonight?" Craig asked. "And if so, what can we do to protect ourselves?"

Gates peered at Craig as if the questions were unexpected. The ghost's gaze seemed unfocused. Craig recalled the "thousand-yard stare" of traumatized soldiers. He'd only heard the term, but now, he felt sure he saw it in the dead man's eyes.

"Dodge Challenger… you know, that's been bugging me for so long I… I…"

"Alva, it's okay," Craig said.

This was more familiar territory. The ghost seeking answers, dwelling in trauma, and confused and lost and alone. He spoke on as Gates rambled with less and less coherence, about Zelda, his early life, and his time in the military. Tara looked on patiently, listening to the one-sided conversation, as Craig coaxed more information out of the long-dead psychic.

After nearly fifteen minutes, Gates seemed to remember where he was. His eyes snapped into focus, and he gave a mirthless bark of laughter.

"Oh my… Sorry fella, was I rambling? This could take all night. I have to keep so many plates spinning, you know? The Five know I'm with you now, and they'll send another discarnate for us unless I keep blocking them… but they're too strong. I get the feeling they still want to scare you off. They don't like to draw attention, but… Hell, I've got an idea, Craig."

Craig started to ask what Gates meant but the ghost interrupted.

"Brace yourself, this might hurt a little."

Gates leaned forward and his forehead merged with Craig's. Craig heard Tara shout something and felt her grab his arm, but the hotel room was already fading as a torrent of strange memories flooded his mind.

A chaos of sensations, sights, words, and emotions overwhelmed him in no chronological order. He tried to cry out, but he was paralyzed. He was being subsumed into Alva Gates, a man of jagged fragments of information held together by sheer egotism and a sense of purpose.

Craig was drowning in another man's memories. He put the pieces in order in some kind of coherent pattern. He found little Alva in school, attention-seeking, clever enough to be funny but not working too hard because he needed to be popular. Next came Alva as a teen, a minor track star with a neat line for the girls. Then Alva Gates got drafted and all was chaos again.

There were hazy memories of basic training, leave, and several young women. One in particular was crying, her elaborate makeup wrecked by tears and mouth distorted by misery. Gates felt shame for the first time, regret even, but Craig had no time to discover more. The swirling vortex of Gates' mind was carrying him onward to a specific place at a fateful moment.

The patrol was at the top of a hill, which was bad because there was no cover, just a few straggly bushes. Some dumbass captain, wet behind the ears, had told them to get up the hill and reconnoiter for VCs. The Vietcong spotted them first, of course, and a sniper had hit Alva's sergeant right in the throat. The man lay gurgling blood onto the red-brown dirt. Then it was like a giant had picked up Gates and thrown him way into the air, maybe ten feet, and let him tumble down the hill.

Gates couldn't hear a damn thing when he finally hit a boulder and stopped rolling. He had survived a hit from the enemy or maybe artillery. The high-explosive round that should have killed him had flung him clear.

Gates didn't have time to savor the irony. Two skinny men in black clothes appeared, running uphill, their rifles aimed at him. In the movies, he'd have shot both of them because the bad guys never react quickly and can't shoot straight, but this wasn't a movie and Gates had no chance. He flung away his carbine and raised his hands, praying they would not kill him.

One of the VCs raised his Kalashnikov, the wooden butt poised to smash Alva's face. The other guerilla snapped out a sharp command, which prompted a brief argument. The rifle was lowered. Using gestures, shoving, and the odd punch, the second guerilla had him moving north. The firing died away. Gates assumed the platoon had been wiped out, as he saw no other captives before they reached a jungle trail and linked up with a dozen or so other VCs.

He was mistaken. His party caught up with another group of guerillas, a dozen or so men with another captive American in an olive-drab uniform. It was Captain Harding, his face dirty, and his eyes wide with fear. The damn fool who'd set them up to fail.

"You idiot," Gates spat.

That earned him a vicious blow from a gun butt in the small of his back.

"No talking."

It was the first time any of his captors had spoken English. The man who had spoken was the VC who had protected Gates earlier. Evidently, he was an officer, or at least the leader of this group.

Gates' memories became chaotic again. Craig felt a terrible foreboding, and the trek through the forest became a patchwork of images and sensations. More blows and more arguments among his captors. A deserted village with most of the huts burned down. About eighty yards beyond the village was a lake with a small island.

On the island was a squat structure, ancient and overgrown. The looming bulk was illuminated by the setting sun. Holes that might have once been doors and windows looked like the apertures in a misshapen skull.

The leader pointed to the ruins as he looked at the Americans. "You go there. Go now."

CHAPTER 21

RUINS

When the two Americans hesitated, the man jerked the barrel of his gun toward the lake.

"Go! Or you die now."

Another VC made a comment in their native language. It prompted laughter, unpleasant to hear, rippling through the group.

"Guess we gotta swim," Gates said resignedly.

He waded out into the reeds, not thinking to take off his boots. He felt his feet sinking into silt as cool water saturated his fatigues up to the waist. He heard the captain behind him, trying to argue or bargain. Then Gates flinched at the sound of rifle fire. Six, maybe seven rounds. He looked around, but the captain was not lying dead in the mud. Instead, the officer splashed clumsily into the water.

Gates was under no illusions about the Vietcong leader's intentions. The ruins on the island might be infested with snakes, scorpions, or other poisonous creatures. Or maybe the VCs would just shoot them halfway across for sport. That seemed more likely to Gates. He had been in Vietnam long enough to know that neither side was fighting a gentleman's war. At around the halfway point, he felt the flesh between his shoulder blades start to itch. Forty yards was easy, even with AKs. But as he grew closer to the island, no shots rang out over the water. When Gates summoned the courage to glance over his shoulder, he saw that the VCs had started a fire. Only a couple of men watched the Americans.

"Why do you think they let us go?" the captain asked. "Why'd they do that?"

"They didn't," Gates replied.

The captain kept on talking, asking dumb questions, but Gates ignored him. He climbed up the muddy bank onto the island, forcing his way through clumps of weeds to reach the ruins. The officer followed, his presence annoying. Up close, the ruins were just a rough rectangle of stone walls that had collapsed in places, but there were no signs of blocks being taken away for reuse despite the village's proximity. The trail he had left through the vegetation was unique. Nothing bigger than a bird had been here in a long while.

Come to think of it, Gates thought, *I can't hear any birds. Or insects.*

Gates stepped across the threshold and into the ruined building. He immediately felt a chill, like the coldest winter rain sleeting through him. He shivered despite the heat, and feeling dizzy, put a hand on the nearest wall. It seemed to leech the warmth from his fingers and palm. He jerked back his hand and turned to leave, only to collide with the captain.

"What is it?" the officer demanded.

"It's bad," Gates said. "It's a bad place. We need to go."

The captain asked more questions, but Gates ignored them. Instead, he moved around until the campfire was out of sight. It was almost pitch dark, with just a sliver of moon. It would be easy to wade across the lake and keep the island between themselves and the VCs.

"Too easy," Gates murmured. "They must know we might do that. So, whatever's going to happen…"

The captain stumbled through the foliage and stood beside him.

"What? I still don't understand. Why did they send us here?"

Gates looked at the vague outline of the man, just visible against the deeper darkness of the time-worn stones. Before he could give an exasperated reply, he noticed a change in the quality of the light. The captain was silhouetted by a faint glow. It came from one of the windows. A steady white light moved inside the ruined building.

"Oh God, there's something here."

Gates wanted to turn and run down to the shore and then wade out to safety, but he was paralyzed by the sight of the light, his feet rooted in the dirt. He saw the captain spin around as the light passed behind him, vanished for a moment, and then reappeared in the doorway. It was brighter now, an orb about four inches across. The captain's face was illuminated by the glow. His expression showed more puzzlement than fear.

Gates made a tremendous effort to look away from the light, which was floating toward them at a walking pace. He managed to lift one foot, take a clumsy step back, and then lost his balance and fell. The captain made a whimpering sound as the light seemed to hesitate, then drift past him. It hovered over Gates. He raised one hand to fend it off, but it passed through his spread fingers. He gave a muffled scream at the intense cold. Then the light flickered and died.

The next thing he knew, it was morning. The captain was gone, but standing over him was the Vietcong leader flanked by two of his men. He could not decipher their expressions, but at least they weren't aiming their AKs at him.

"You are still alive," said the leader. "I did not expect that."

"Sorry to disappoint you," he muttered, raising onto one elbow.

"I am not disappointed," said the leader, hunkering down by Gates. "Merely surprised."

Gates waited for the man to say something else. Instead, the VC stood up and said something rapidly to his men. They looked relieved and were soon wading back to their camp.

"They are superstitious peasants from this area," the leader explained. "They say the island is haunted."

"It is," Gates said, looking his enemy in the eye. "I saw it. Whatever *it* is."

The VC shrugged.

"The ghost of an evil magician who lived on the island—so the story goes. They say that some survive his touch and gain great powers. But such men always die a terrible death."

Gates had nothing to say to that. The VC looked back at the campsite. His men were preparing to move out. To Gates' surprise, the man took a U.S. military compass out of a pocket and handed it over.

"We have a long march ahead of us and our rations are low, so we cannot take prisoners. You may go south while we go north. Perhaps you will find your comrades. But you will probably die. It is the nature of war."

The VC left without another word. Gates watched him wade back to shore and vanish into the jungle with his company. He checked the compass and saw that his route would take him through the deserted village. He waded back to shore, taking out a Hershey bar that his captors had missed when they'd frisked him.

As he ate, he became aware of movement among the burned huts. Panic seized him at the thought that his captors might be returning, or maybe a different group. But then he saw that the people emerging from what remained of the huts were civilians. There were youngsters and old people, a pregnant woman, and another woman carrying a little child. No men of fighting age. No sign of weapons.

Gates threw down the wrapper of the Hershey bar and raised a hand in welcome. He called out a couple of the Vietnamese phrases he'd been taught. He told them he was a friend, and that he would not hurt them. More than a dozen villagers lined up in a semicircle just out of reach. None of them spoke. They had been hiding, from one side or maybe both.

Gates began to repeat his reassuring words, hoping he wasn't mangling them too badly to be understood. A skinny little girl ran forward, picked up the candy wrapper, and held it up to him. No translation was required. He shook his head, smiling ruefully, and crouched to bring his face level with hers. It was imperative not to scare these people.

"I'm sorry, honey. I only had the one."

The girl frowned, ran toward him, and held out her hand. As soon as she came close, hunger flooded through Gates, a ravenous need that blotted out all other feelings. And it was not just hunger. He saw, against the backdrop of jungle and sky, a green-clad giant whose face was a reddish mass of grotesque, massive features.

He was seeing himself through the child's eyes.

Gates jumped up and took a pace backward. The raging hunger and the bizarre vision vanished. The child cried out in disappointment and stamped a bare foot on the red-brown dirt. An old man pointed at the island, rattling off a series of questions. Gates shook his head, trying to indicate that he didn't understand. Whatever the man was saying scared the villagers. The pregnant woman rushed forward and dragged the little girl away. Then the people retreated past the remains of their homes to vanish into the trees.

CHAPTER 22
PSYCHIC SCHTICK

Alva Gates somehow found his way home. The details were hazy, as the man's mind struggled with so many conflicting impressions. Telepathy, the unwanted and baffling power, certainly proved useful. He could not only sense humans nearby but also animals, and avoided danger instinctively despite being fatigued and traumatized. He was rescued by a patrol from another unit, sent back to the base suffering from exhaustion and dehydration, and then ended up in a military psychiatric facility in California. He was given powerful medication at first because he kept insisting that he was a telepath thanks to encountering a long-dead Vietnamese sorcerer.

He was released from the army and sent to a civilian hospital after a few weeks. The diagnosis was psychosis brought on by combat fatigue. That was in 1971. He spent the next three years undergoing treatment, including electroconvulsive therapy.

This phase in Gates' life story was almost as traumatic for Craig as it had been for Gates. Trapped in the slipstream of a war veteran's fractured mind, he could only spectate. But he was not just an onlooker.

He shared Gates' sufferings at every level. He felt the needles go into his arm, the sedatives course through his veins, the tender mercies of the orderlies, and the terrible humiliation, rage, and fear. He felt the terror that had washed over Gates when they put the rubber-coated metal bar between his teeth and the moist pads on the sides of his head. He felt the shocks go through his brain. Above all, he felt despair and boredom, and the misery of a world of hard-eyed strangers and closed doors.

Gates learned early on not to claim he could read minds, but that didn't help much. He was surrounded by people that radiated all kinds of crazy. He felt sympathy for them, of course. But their illnesses became his as he could not shut it out. His nightmares blurred into waking dreams that wore him out and made him incoherent and confused. The only way he could have recovered was to be released, but that could never happen. Gates had read *Catch-22* just before his call-up and found it amusing. Now, he was living it.

Alva Gates might have been locked up for the rest of his life, or at least for another decade or so. But he eventually learned to tune out most of the dark thoughts that emanated from the other patients. It was a skill he acquired through necessity. Until one day, a doctor told him he was going home.

"I don't have a home," Gates said. "My mom is dead, and my dad—hell, I don't know where he is. I got no other family, Doc."

The doctor said that was a pity. Then he startled Gates with an idea.

"Look, I can't say this officially, but… I've seen some of those early interviews. I don't know if you can read minds. Officially, I don't believe in such powers. But even if it is just a trick, why not use it when you get out? I hate to see traumatized vets ending up on Skid Row."

Gates stared at him, sensing quite clearly that the man was sincere and not pandering to a supposed delusion. They were sitting on the floor of an actual padded cell.

"You think I should—what? Take my act on the road or something? Join a circus?"

The doctor shrugged and started to say something. But suddenly, Gates got a strong mental image from the man that was both shocking and weirdly appealing. The doctor was in a room with two other doctors and three attractive women. All were more or less naked, though one of the doctors was still wearing socks with suspenders.

Gates found all this so distracting that he had to ask the psychiatrist to repeat his advice.

"You could go to Vegas and do a mind-reading act," the doctor said.

It wasn't that simple, of course. After the friendly psychiatrist got him released, Gates had to readjust to normal life. Except that life could never be normal again, not for a true mind reader. Even the simplest transaction like buying chips at the corner store was fraught with pitfalls. The little old lady behind him in the queue might be contemplating poisoning her neighbor's cat. The girl at the checkout might find Gates creepy, smiling and joking with him all the while.

Once or twice, Gates was overwhelmed by the horrors of other people's minds. He accidentally dipped into the thoughts of a killer once, thanks to a crowded bus turning a sharp corner. He brushed up against a skinny little guy in overalls carrying a toolbox. The man was thinking about the special tools he carried and what he was going to do with them. Variations on what he had already done many times.

Gates almost threw up on a woman carrying a sleeping baby and rushed to get off at the next stop. He dry-heaved by the road for a while before thinking of calling the cops. But what could he tell them about the man with the toolbox? He could barely remember the guy's face. The faces of his victims were all too vivid, though. For days, he hesitated before deciding that he would not be believed.

Instead, Alva Gates decided to earn a living as a real psychic and let the world take care of its myriad problems without him. He learned to hustle a little, cultivate a more extroverted personality, and become a showman. He found a niche at a carnival as the "Amazing Alva, Mind Reader Extraordinaire". The owner of the carnival didn't care if Gates was genuine, just that he pulled in the crowds. It was almost too easy. He walked into a tent and sensed the most powerful mental emanations, usually from someone in the first two or three rows. Then he carefully selected a target, almost always a woman who would be surprised and pleased to be told a few innocent facts about themselves. He avoided men, as a rule, as they could turn belligerent.

"You, madam. Yes, the lovely lady in the red coat. How's Eric doing?"

The response was usually open-mouthed surprise.

"Eric is your son, currently in… Baltimore, I believe? Training as some kind of electrician? You seem a little vague about the actual job."

This kind of direct hit in the first minute of the act impressed all but the most die-hard skeptics. And Alva was always careful to give those skeptics a kind of escape route, modeling his act on several he'd checked out before getting started. He did the old one where someone wrote a phrase on a piece of paper, out of Alva's sight of course, then put it into an envelope. Alva read the phrase in their minds, of course, but went through the rigmarole of slapping the envelope onto his forehead before revealing it.

Eventually, he ran into a talent scout from Atlantic City who offered him a gig at a casino hotel. It wasn't quite Vegas, but Alva accepted, bought himself a new outfit, and headed for the East Coast.

That was in the mid-70s. In Atlantic City, he learned a lot about showbiz from other acts while fending off questions from stage magicians. Not one even hinted at real psychic powers, which was interesting.

By 1975, the Amazing Alva had an agent and a six-month run in Vegas. He had also acquired a slight paunch, a fake tan, a lot of jewelry, and a Dodge Challenger with real Morocco leather upholstery. Publicity stunts followed. Gates drove blindfolded right through the garish overlit heart of the city. He steered Zelda along the strip, past Caesar's Palace with a reporter from a national TV network in the passenger seat. Gates saw through the reporter's eyes, so he could have gone at a normal speed, but that would have looked fake. Gates realized early on that it didn't pay to do seemingly impossible things too easily, so Zelda crawled along at about fifteen miles per hour while Gates gave a continuous commentary to the reporter on how hard it was to stay focused. This ensured that his show was sold out for the entire run, one that extended to eighteen months.

The Amazing Alva was suddenly famous. Maybe not Elvis famous, but Ringo Starr level. Things were looking good. He used his powers to get lots of sex, felt ashamed, and kept doing it anyway. After all, he could genuinely claim he knew what women wanted. As one girl told him, "You're kind of a creep sometimes, but it's like you read my mind."

"Yeah," he'd said. "I get that a lot."

And then the good times ended.

One Tuesday night, Gates was walking to his car when a short guy ran up to him. Gates had never thought about hiring security, but the expression on the man's face made him regret that choice. The alley where he'd parked was indirectly lit by neon spilling in from the Strip. Even in that uncertain light, he could see the guy's expression was dead, emotionless.

"Hey, do I know you?" he asked without looking, stepping closer to Zelda, and taking out his keys.

Then Gates sensed waves of despair and loneliness from the man. It was another veteran, down on his luck. He was reaching into his pocket for some loose change when the other man spoke and immediately stopped being a stranger.

"Gates, you don't remember me?"

Then he remembered.

"Captain Harding?"

Anger flared up, so sudden and intense that it scared Gates a little. He raised his fist. The car keys protruded between his fingers. He almost smashed the metal points into the other man's face. Harding flinched but didn't step back or try to protect himself. His hands stayed by his side.

"Go ahead," Harding said. "I deserve it."

Gates calmed down a little.

"You aren't seriously panhandling me right now?" Gates asked. "I mean, it would be in character, you whiny jerk, but you won't get a penny—"

"No!" Harding radiated anger now, like a flash of lightning.

Gates was a lot of things, but vindictive was not one of them. He felt his resentment for the captain ebbing away. He opened the door of his car.

"Get in," he said. "Let's drive and talk, it helps me get things straight in my head."

Gates felt relief emanating from Harding as they set off into the near-midnight traffic. As they drove around Vegas, he learned about a town he'd never heard of, and people he didn't know. He heard about a terrible darkness looming over the lives of thousands of good people. And the Amazing Alva thought back to that guy on the bus with the toolbox. The killer he'd done nothing to stop.

Craig was still observing all this, and still powerless to intervene. He had guessed who Harding was at the same moment as Gates. When the retired captain started talking about ghosts, he was not surprised.

"They tell me things, Gates," Harding said. "At first, I thought I was imagining them, but it was that thing in the ruins, the light. It opened some kind of inner eye. It did the same for you, right? That's how you do your act?"

Gates explained that, no, his unwanted gift was of a different kind.

"Tell me more about the ghosts," he urged. "What's up with them?"

Harding struggled to explain.

"They know something evil is rising in Grendon Mill," he said. "It makes them jumpy. They kind of vanish and then reappear, unlike regular ghosts. It's black magic or something. But they agree there's a group of five powerful individuals behind it."

"And you came all the way to Nevada to tell me about it?" Gates asked. "Why? If there's some kind of Satanist conspiracy or whatever, why not tell the police?"

There was a long silence as Harding just kept staring up at Gates. They stopped at a traffic light and a party of drunken tourists reeled across, shouting and waving at the guys in the fancy car. Then Gates chuckled.

"Yeah, that was a dumb question. The cops wouldn't listen."

"One of them is the police chief," Harding said flatly. "There's the mayor, the school principal, and I think another one is a youth pastor. Not sure. The ghosts aren't very clear. The Five seem to have some kind of psychic shield that protects them when they gather. They've got this thing—an amulet. It gives them power, lets them do all kinds of weird stuff. Mess with people's minds."

"Wow."

Gates hit the gas as the lights changed, swung off the Strip, and circled the center of town. Craig listened, powerless to withdraw or intervene, as the men talked some more.

"You've got to come, Gates," Harding said. "I know you have good cause to despise me. But innocent people are at risk, I'm sure. Well, the ghosts are sure. And they won't leave me alone, so I thought with your powers—"

"I get it," Gates cut in. "What the hell, I'll check it out. But if you're wasting my time, or this is some kind of scam…"

"It isn't. Swear to God."

CHAPTER 23
THE SPIRIT OF SEVENTY-SIX

At first, Grendon Mill seemed like just another sleepy New England town to Alva Gates. He found it nice if a little dull. He checked in to a B&B and wandered around for a day, taking in the colorful clapboard houses, dinky little stores, and big-city tourists hiking the woods or fishing in the river.

But then he started reading the townsfolk and getting disconcerting waves of thought and emotion. Things had been heard, glimpsed, and guessed at. Something was going down at the old mill upriver. It was a place best avoided; everyone knew that. The kids made up stories about it, but none of them went near it after dark. There were no dares in Grendon Mill, only a self-imposed curfew for just about everybody.

Gates chatted with people and was delighted to be recognized by a New York couple. He was a minor celebrity, and that felt good. He gave them his autograph. They and the other tourists he encountered had none of the anxieties of the locals. This supported some of Captain Harding's story, as he told the man that evening in Dinah's Diner.

"That was a good steak," Gates said, leaning back and lighting a cigarette. "Any ghosts in here?"

Harding shook his head.

"They sense something bad coming and they're agitated, trying to get away."

Gates skimmed the surface of Harding's mind and found he was telling the truth. That was what bothered him. He knew nothing about ghosts but felt they ought to be kind of scary. If scary things got scared, that was bad.

"Okay," he said, jabbing his cigarette for emphasis. "I accept that something is going on, but I still haven't got any hint of this Five even existing. Just some stuff about the old lumber mill."

Harding leaned forward across the table.

"Lower your voice," he hissed. "One of them is coming in right now."

Gates did not make the mistake of staring at the newcomer as the door of the diner opened. He'd seen enough movies and shows about private eyes to know better. He acted normal and glanced up, feigning mild interest. He saw a tall woman of about forty with shoulder-length blonde hair. She was dressed soberly and carrying a folder and some books.

Harding whispered urgently.

"Mary Baker. She's the school principal."

The woman walked along the room of booths and Gates caught her eye, giving her a not-too-big smile. She raised an eyebrow, and the corners of her mouth twitched. Now that he had focused her attention on him, Gates reached out to detect her thoughts. There was nothing unusual, just a recognition that a man—probably a tourist—found her attractive. She got closer, and he was able to go a little deeper.

Mary Baker's mind was superficially normal, the kind Gates had scanned many times. But beneath the surface of career and small-town socializing lay something else. There was ambition coupled with a cold ruthlessness that made Gates flinch. There were flashes of memory, of robed figures in animal masks, chanting, and a sense of elation. And then, at the center of it all, a dagger plunged into the helpless body of a girl who could not have been more than fifteen.

That was only the beginning of the vile ritual.

Gates ran clumsily from the booth, hand over his mouth, into the diner's washroom. He just made it to the toilet in time. He spent the next few minutes puking up steak, onions, fries, and coffee. Harding appeared, nervous at the attention they had drawn but genuinely concerned for Gates.

When he was sure he was just dry-heaving, Gates got off his knees and flushed.

"I believe you now, Harding," he managed to say. "These people— they have to be stopped."

That night, in Gates' chintzy room at the B&B, they talked over their options. They could not call the cops because the police chief was one of The Five. He knew enough to make every one of the murders a perfect crime. The FBI would probably dismiss them as hoaxers. Even if they believed them, the first thing the bureau would do was contact the local cops anyway.

"We have to take them out ourselves," Gates insisted.

He sensed Harding's hesitation, the cowardice mingled with foolhardiness that had doomed so many men in Vietnam. This was not the ally Gates would have chosen, but they had to act quickly because before nausea and horror had overcome him, Gates had picked up another fact from the depraved mind of Mary Baker.

"Can't we do something else?" Harding asked plaintively. "The Five play for keeps, and we're outnumbered."

Gates spelled out why they had to act. In just four days, a great ritual would be performed. It was the first phase, leading to an ultimate sacrifice on the third night. The victim was to be a perfect innocent—a sweet, innocent child whose trust Mary Baker had cultivated. The process would summon something monstrous and powerful to Grendon Mill. Gates didn't care much for the whys and wherefores, he only knew that he had to save the child and stop whatever it was from breaking through into their world.

"We've got to kill them," he said. "Kill them all. It's the only way."

Suddenly, Craig lost all sense of the co-memories he was experiencing. They started to become less coherent and were no longer sequential. It was a recurrence of the psychotic break Gates had suffered in Vietnam. The journey east, the meeting with Harding, the arrival in Grendon Mill—all were jumbled. And there was something else. A looming horror at the core of a wounded mind. Something walled up but not quite secure.

The death of Alva Gates.

Craig knew he had to see it. He must know how it happened because everything else that mattered—The Five, the ritual, the final confrontation—was behind that blank wall that seemed to stretch to infinity in all directions. For the first time, he communicated with the dead psychic.

"Alva. Let me in."

There was no response, only more fragmentary memories and pangs of pain and fear. Craig persisted, reaching out as best he could, trying to send a message of hope and compassion.

"Let me in, Alva."

And the ghost let him in.

Craig saw what had been behind that wall and knew he could not face it, could never face it. He tried to scream, to struggle, to back away, but an insatiable dark vortex drew him into the violent death of Alva Gates. A death that was only the beginning of Gates' suffering. The attack on the cultists, the gunfire and the flames, the snatching of the amulet from the leader—all of these things were almost trivial compared to what came after.

Craig experienced Gates' agony as one of the dying killers drove a ceremonial dagger into his side. He felt contempt and rage as Gates saw Harding running from the blazing building. He suffered with Gates as the man ran from the lumber mill, clutching the amulet, into the woods. The amulet seemed to pulse in his hand, channeling strange power through his body. He grasped instinctively that it was interacting with the gift Gates had been given on an island thousands of miles away. That it was, in a sense, becoming one with him. That his death was a kind of ritual sacrifice, an unwitting process that summoned whatever entity slumbered in the amulet.

Gates found a hiding place and burrowed under vast, ancient tree roots like a wounded animal. There he lay, one hand clutching his wound, and the other clasping the amulet. His vision was failing as the sun gave the first hint of color in the sky. And then, Alva Gates was dead.

Craig shared the man's surprise as he stood over his own corpse.

And then Alva Gates' true ordeal began.

CHAPTER 24

BACK IN THE ROOM

"What happened?"

A pale-faced woman was leaning over him. Craig realized he was lying on the floor, which was embarrassing. Had he passed out? Was this the end of another terrible date? If so, it was a pity. The young woman was quite attractive in an intense sort of way. But she was slapping his face a little too hard.

"Please stop," he mumbled.

"Craig?" the woman said, louder now. "Craig, are you with me? Can you tell me what year it is?"

"Nineteen seventy…" he began. "No, it's not. Sorry."

He managed to remember the right year and let her help him sit up. He remembered her name. Tara. They were not on a date, which was a relief. Then he recalled what they were doing and anxiety reasserted itself. He glanced around the room. Gates was gone.

"How long was I out?"

"About half a minute," said Tara, helping him onto the sofa. "Maybe a little longer. I was getting worried."

Craig stared at her as she sat beside him.

"What… half a minute? It seemed like years. I got all of Gates' memories—well, most of them. Kind of like the Vulcan mind meld, you know?"

That prompted a quick smile from her.

"Nerds of the world unite," she said. "Okay, so what did this 'melding' accomplish?"

He gave a sequential account, but it wasn't easy. He had a feeling that facts were slipping away, like the details of a vivid dream that faded with the morning light. He couldn't find words to convey just how terrifying the thought of that island had been. Even now, remembering the dead man's memory—which was weird enough—Craig shuddered.

"Sounds like an old-school curse that gave Gates his wild talent," Tara mused. "Sometimes, a traumatic event uncovers paranormal powers. But in this case, they were kind of grafted on. Nasty."

"Yeah, but that's not the main thing," Craig said. "I found out who brought Gates here. I saw his face—'twas kind of distinctive. And his voice hasn't changed that much."

"Cappy?" Tara asked.

"Yeah."

"I knew it!" she exclaimed. "Right, we track him down tomorrow and pump him for information. Nothing about the new victim? Why they're killing runaways?"

"Not really," Craig said. "Gates' memories are clearest when he's recalling his early life. There's a clear progression of events, a story he can tell. I think he wanted me to know who he was, his origin story. He's got a huge ego."

"You don't say," Tara grinned. "But he should have told you more about what happened when he got here, right?"

As Craig explained what he'd sensed, Tara's frustration was evident but her voice indicated sympathy.

"I guess his death was so terrible that he can't face it, even after all these years as a ghost."

Craig was not so sure.

"I've talked to a lot of ghosts, and some had pretty horrendous deaths. But there's something special about Gates. I mean, okay, there's lots that's special. But on top of that. Something walled off. Except… I kind of remember passing through that wall somehow. But all I got on the other side was—"

He closed his eyes and clutched his forehead.

"Oh God, it's coming back now. I guess... I guess my mind blocked it out... but... oh God."

The memory flooded through Craig, and the hotel room vanished. He heard Tara's voice, a distant, fading sound. He felt something gripping his arm, his shoulder. But there was too much fear and pain. He lay on a slab in the woods with masked people standing over him. He was tied down. The robed figure in the owl mask produced an old-fashioned straight razor.

"All you have to do is tell us where it is, Alva."

The words came from a snake mask, close to his ear.

He looked down at his body as the razor-wielding cultists made a diagonal cut across his abdomen. Except that it was not his body. It was that of an adolescent girl.

"Tell us where it is."

The razor moved lower, cold steel easily parting flesh, blood flowing copiously now.

"We mustn't do too much damage," said a woman's voice.

"Craig!"

Tara was shaking him violently. Even in his confusion, he wondered if she worked out.

"Craig, stop passing out on me, please."

"I'm okay," he said. "I just had a flashback, kind of. It's a great big memory salad. God, I had no idea this kind of thing was possible."

She let go of his shoulders and sat back.

"You'd be surprised by what's possible, Craig. Tell me what you've discovered."

Craig told her. Back in 1976, Gates had used his powers to determine that the original Five were going to summon up some ancient, probably demonic, power. Their motives were the usual—power, wealth, long lives, smiting their enemies. And their means of achieving the summoning was the amulet.

"Describe it, please," she begged. "At least so we'll know it if we see it."

"It's kind of diamond-shaped—like the diamonds in a deck of cards, you know?" he replied. "The metal might be silver or some alloy of silver. It's definitely not gold. Gates saw it for a few moments, worn around the neck of the leader. Once he'd identified The Five, he found it easy to get close enough to read them."

Craig stopped, closed his eyes, and ran his fingers over his forehead.

"The things they did. Depraved, vile—but always with a purpose. Ritual murders, systematic, always preying on the innocent and naïve. The weak. It was culminating in a ceremony at the old lumber mill at midnight. But Gates and Cappy worked out a plan. They couldn't call the cops, obviously, with the police chief involved. So, they decided on murder."

For the first time, Tara looked shocked.

"They snuck into the building and hid cans of gasoline around the place. They had guns. The idea was to shoot The Five, burn down the mill, and end it all there. But Cappy had chickened out at the last minute. He'd set the place on fire and ran, leaving Gates to tackle The Five and stop them from getting out."

"He got four of them," Tara prompted as Craig fell silent.

"Yeah, but the leader got close enough to stab him. Gates wounded the guy, took the amulet, and ran for the woods. He knew he was bleeding out, so he wanted to hide the damn thing because he couldn't destroy it."

Craig paused again.

"I think it's alive, Tara. The amulet. There's some kind of intelligence in there, a powerful entity. It started to… infect? Is that the word? It started to merge with Gates in some way as he fled. Maybe Gates being on the verge of death had something to do with it. Or maybe it's his abilities. He hid in the woods, still clutching the amulet, and died. His ghost still has his psychic power and more. I'm kind of hazy on that part."

"And he's been safeguarding the amulet ever since," Tara added. "But he didn't tell you where it is?"

Craig shook his head.

"Great," she said.

"That's not the worst of it," Craig said. "I found out what they did to the discarnates."

CHAPTER 25

THE DISCARNATES

"For years," Craig said, "Gates tried to stop the surviving member of The Five from reforming his cult. But it wasn't easy. The guy still had power, and Gates' influence doesn't extend far into town."

"Who was this survivor?" Tara asked. "He must be really old by now."

"He's dead now," Craig explained. "He was old then, but he died back in the eighties. But by that time, he'd already found new recruits, God knows how. There must always be five members, for some reason. It's been the rule in Grendon Mill from the start. The point is that, with his added power from the amulet, Gates could fend them off. He could cloud their minds and stop them from finding his body. Deny them the one thing they needed."

"But surely they could just search the woods," Tara objected. "Maybe invent some pretext—lost treasure, something like that?"

"Yes, they did, but Gates arranged a few incidents. People getting spooked, dogs going berserk. He managed to lure a bear down from the hills once, scared the crap out of a search party. After that, The Five searched quietly as a group. But by then, Gates had set up some kind of paranormal barrier. He got the feeling the amulet didn't want to be found by those guys. That it was seeking someone else. Not him, but someone."

"Makes sense," Tara mused. "Magical objects sometimes have minds of their own. And this one's held by the ghost of a psychic. Wow, it's quite the combination. So, they ended up with a kind of Mexican standoff, with neither side able to defeat the other?"

"That was the situation… at first," Craig said. "But then, The Five came up with a plan. The incalling."

Tara frowned.

"Never heard of it. Some kind of ritual, I'm guessing?"

"It's one of the most horrible things—" Craig began, but then broke off as Gates walked through the hotel room door. "He's back."

"I am indeed," said the ghost, with a grin that glinted with gold. *"And I bring bad tidings. Another attack is coming, kids, so be prepared. I'll do my best to fend them off, but I'm spinning… spinning a lot of plates…"*

Gates' garish clothes faded to a near monochrome, and Craig saw through the ghost. He began to warn Tara, but she was already standing with a dagger in each hand. Craig grabbed the air pistol on the bedside table. He was still fumbling with it when the first ghost appeared.

The discarnate was surprisingly small. Crouching, it scuttled from the shadows like a spider, its blurred mouth emitting a pitiful moaning. Craig pointed the BB gun at it, but Tara slashed blindly at the same time. It was on her in an instant, wrapping dark limbs around her legs and torso. She yelled and brought the daggers down by instinct. One iron blade entered the thing's head and it sprang aside, howling. Craig aimed and sent an iron pellet through the ghost. It shattered the mirror that was set into the closet door.

The discarnate retreated a few steps before vanishing.

"Gone!" Craig shouted, then regretted his haste.

Gates wrestled with at least two other attackers by the door, their smoky limbs wrapped around him. Craig aimed but hesitated, unsure what would happen if he shot Gates.

"Are there more? Talk to me, Craig," Tara demanded.

"He's fighting them," Craig said, pointing toward the door. "Don't attack."

Craig then saw an opening and fired again. The shot passed through the discarnates and struck the door with a loud bang. One of the killer ghosts writhed and retreated into the corridor. The other flailed its disproportioned limbs in rage and then advanced toward the bed.

"Right in front," Craig snapped as he recharged his pistol.

Tara dropped her daggers.

"What the hell?" Craig shouted.

But the daggers had not struck the floor. Instead, they hovered just a couple of feet above the carpet. Then they whirled diagonally upward toward the ghost, dodging and weaving in a bizarre aerobatic display. Tara stood, head down, eyes closed, and fists clenched at her side. The fast-moving blades spun back and forth, impossible to dodge, creating a zone of pain for the discarnate. The thing screeched so piercingly that Craig's ears hurt. But after several passes from the flying knives, the attacker had had enough. It danced back, waving its overly long arms in distress. Then it shrank to a black point and vanished.

"They're gone." Craig was incredulous.

Tara opened her eyes and sighed.

"Long time since I had to do that. Still got it, though."

She sat down on the bed heavily, even paler than usual. Craig wondered how much energy psychokinesis drew from the mind and body. He decided not to ask but instead babbled out his thanks.

"Couldn't have done it without you," she said, smiling up at him. "You're the best seer I've worked with."

There was a scream from the corridor before Craig could reply, and he remembered the ghost that had fled. He rushed outside to see a white-haired woman in pajamas kneeling beside a stocky man lying on his back. There was no sign of any ghosts. The door of the room next door was open. More doors opened and guests emerged, tetchy and bleary-eyed.

Craig guessed that the old guy had collided with the retreating discarnate. It had probably not been a full-on attack. There was still a chance. Tara ran to the couple. She asked questions about the man's health, checked his pulse, and then gave him CPR. The man's wife looked on, her face glistening with tears. Craig knelt beside Tara. He saw no sign of the old man's ghost.

"I think it's working," he said quietly.

A member of hotel staff appeared, a young woman who was presumably the night manager. There were attempted explanations, but as the man came around, no blame seemed to attach to Craig and Tara. They helped carry the man to the bed in his room and then retreated, leaving the corridor to gossips and gawkers.

"That was close," Craig said as he shut the door. "He was probably coming to complain about the noise. Innocent bystander."

"Well, we helped," Tara pointed out. "And there are other innocents in danger. One in particular; the kid about to be sacrificed."

They sat again, he on the bed and she on the sofa facing him.

"Now," she said. "What were you going to tell me about the discarnates?"

Craig took a breath.

"The Five decided the only way they could get the location of the amulet from Gates was to torture it out of him."

"But he's a ghost," Tara said. "Oh…"

Craig saw the beginnings of understanding dawn in her eyes.

"I didn't believe it at first, but I experienced it," he said. "They found a way of inserting Gates' spirit into a living body. A kind of forcible possession—the incalling, they call it. And then they torture him and the living person together. To try and get him to give up the amulet."

Tara looked genuinely shocked for the first time since they'd met.

"They lure runaways here for that?"

Craig forced himself to remember some of the details.

"They displace the soul of the victim. Not completely, though. It stays near the body, trying to get back, confused and horrified. Discarnate. Deprived of a body before its time. It witnesses Gates being tortured. Gates is a fighter, and he never gives in, but it's taken its toll on his mind. They've been trying for decades. They don't seem to have any other plan, like they're obsessed."

"And when the body dies," Tara said slowly, "their spirit becomes deformed and insane, not a regular ghost. That's the vilest thing I've heard in a long while."

A familiar voice spoke from behind Craig's left ear.

"Imagine how I feel."

"Man," Craig moaned. "Don't do that!"

CHAPTER 26

INTO THE WOODS AGAIN

"He's back, right?" Tara asked.

"Yep," Craig said as Gates stood between the two living humans. "And he's not looking great."

Gates was showing some of the scars from his many deaths by torture. As Craig watched, the vicious wounds and burns vanished, along with rips and tears in Gates' gaudy clothes.

"Had a bit of a tussle with those poor sonsofbitches," Gates explained. *"Okay now, but it sent me through the old agonizing death cycle a few times."*

The ghost paused, hands on his hips, and looked around at the damage to the hotel room. Aside from the shattered mirror and a dent in the door, one of Tara's flying daggers was embedded in the back of a chair.

"Well, at least you didn't throw the TV out the window. Saw plenty of that in Vegas from those crummy rock bands. Give me some Johnny Cash any day."

Craig didn't bother repeating that for Tara. Gates perched on the arm of the sofa and looked down at her.

"Telekinesis, huh? Never saw that before. Could be a decisive factor. We've gotta rescue the kid they're keeping in the woods, Craig. And the way I see it…"

Their slow and stilted discussion resumed. It took about an hour to bring Tara up to speed on Gates' ideas, despite Craig getting the knack of condensing Gates' sentences. There was some haggling over details, but not over the need to act.

Gates believed that The Five were going to make a move against the two investigators.

"Halloran could make up some reason to run you out of town," he warned.

"He's done it before with people snooping around the mill ruins. You know how it is in a small town: There's nobody to appeal to. Locals are too scared, and nobody else cares much. And the discarnates are still a real threat. So, if they can't get you one way, they might do it another."

Once she'd heard this, Tara was all for rescuing the runaway right then. Craig argued that they'd be blundering around in the dark, but Gates backed Tara.

"Strike while the iron is hot," Gates said. *"We've beaten back the discarnates. The Five will know and try something else. But it's late, and they've not gotten much sleep. That undermines their power. They need shuteye like the rest of you living people."*

Craig had to smile at the thought of a vicious cult member tucked up in bed like a regular Joe. Then he wondered what Halloran and the others might be dreaming about, and it stopped being funny.

"Okay," he said. "Let's go for it."

Craig peeked outside and saw that the corridor was empty for now. People were talking in the next room. The route to the elevator would take them past the elderly couple's door, which was open. The stairs were in the opposite direction, though, so they picked up their gear and set off. The night manager was not at the front desk, so they left without being seen. An ambulance appeared just as Tara was starting her Discovery.

"Hope the old guy's all right," Craig said.

"He'll be fine," Gates said from the back seat. *"Let's focus on the plan of attack."*

The plan was simple enough. They would drive to the milestone. Tara would go to the cabin and free the captive while Craig and Gates distracted the discarnates. Once the runaway was freed, Tara would pick up Craig, take the youngster to the next town, and contact their folks. Then they would recover the amulet. The plan had obvious flaws. Tara couldn't see the discarnates. The Five might be at the cabin right now. As Gates pointed out, *"No plan of attack survives contact with the enemy."* Craig could have done without that pearl of wisdom but said nothing.

"We keep in touch with the walkies," Tara said. "If it all goes pear-shaped, we regroup either at the milestone or the hotel."

No other vehicles were at the milestone, which was a relief. Craig and Tara set off along the trail, Craig in front with his flashlight aimed downward. Gates agreed to do a recon and vanished. Now and again, they stopped, and Craig switched off his flashlight.

Nothing unusual happened, but he got increasingly jumpy. The absence of sound from birds or animals was far more apparent in the dark.

Gates reappeared and told Craig that the discarnates were drifting aimlessly around the cabin. They couldn't get inside because the cabin was protected by a number of barriers. Some involved incantation, but there was also a simple line of salt that was renewed periodically. None of these would stop a living person.

"Good to know," Tara said when Craig relayed this. "Okay, you guys go and lure the buggers away."

It wasn't difficult to get the attention of the deranged ghosts. The next time Craig turned off his flashlight, he saw pale faces moving among the trees. Soon, there were moans and howls as the phantoms became aware of intruders. According to Gates, the discarnates beaten back at the hotel would be fairly harmless for some time, but that still left several who were, so to speak, fully charged. However, among them was Nikki, Chloe's friend, who had not harmed Craig when she'd had the chance.

"Okay, let's do this," Craig said, moving the flashlight to his left hand and taking out an iron dagger.

Gates was already moving, seeming to phase in and out of existence as he darted back and forth in front of the distorted figures. Gates had been clear about his limitations. He could defeat individual discarnates, but three or more would beat him back. At the moment, only two seemed to be closing in on their party. Craig told Tara, who gave a terse acknowledgment.

"Just let me know when I can run to the cabin," she added.

Craig and Gates worked together. The dead psychic baited their opponents, taunting them with some spicy language that had a vintage feel to it. Craig wondered if some of the insults were more baffling than offensive to the dead youngsters, but it had the desired effect. Two discarnates closed in on Gates, and he grappled with them, the cursing of the psychic mingling with the weird howling and whining of the attackers.

Craig jabbed at the two and managed to drive one away. The second was more tenacious, but between them, he and Gates neutralized it. However, more discarnates had appeared amid the trees. Gates gestured to Craig, and they set off into the woods at a right angle to the trail. Tara, meanwhile, kept going at a brisk jog. She spun two daggers in the air around her, showing remarkable control and making it virtually impossible for any ghost to get past the orbiting knives.

"She's good," Gates observed.

Let's hope she's good enough, Craig thought.

Two pursuers dogged Craig's steps as they doubled back toward the path, planning to head for the road. They hoped to wear down the attackers with a long chase, and it seemed to be working. The discarnates were persistent, but they didn't launch coordinated attacks. Instead, they came at the pair in twos and threes. Gates repelled them with kung fu-like kicks and blows. Craig did his best to assist, slashing at the flailing, elongated limbs.

By the time the trees began to thin out, four or five discarnates were shadowing Craig but keeping out of reach. Their cries were plaintive, almost unbearable. They, too, were victims, enslaved by The Five in death. Craig was almost sure that one of the ghosts was Nikki, Chloe's friend. The specter was smaller than the others and had not attacked them. But the compulsion was still there, and Nikki had to follow them, moaning plaintively.

CHAPTER 27
TURNAROUND

They burst out of the woods and crossed the road. According to Gates, they were on the extreme limit of the discarnates' range. The idea was to lure them here, as far from Tara as possible, then retrace their steps, fighting off the weakened ghosts. Then, they would rendezvous with Tara and the runaway, and escort them back to the car.

The first thing Craig noticed was the police car parked behind Tara's Discovery. The second was Halloran and his deputy, carefully spaced out, hands on their holstered guns. Halloran raised his left hand as Craig pointed the flashlight at him.

"Do not shine that in my eyes," the cop warned.

Craig lowered the beam. The pursuing ghosts were no longer visible, and he couldn't hear them. They had vanished seconds after Craig had stepped onto the road. Gates was still present, though. Craig half expected the ghost to attack Halloran, but Gates seemed confused instead, standing a few feet from Craig and looking on.

"Drop that knife, son," Halloran ordered. "Just drop it. No sudden moves."

Craig hesitated. It was his one defense. The deputy slowly drew his gun but did not point it. Craig dropped the knife, thinking the clink as metal struck the road must have been audible for a hundred yards. Could ghosts hear the way humans did? Craig wished he knew the answer, but it had never seemed important before.

"Carrying a weapon around the woods in the dark seems kind of suspicious to me," Halloran went on. "Now, why don't you just put your hands on that fancy car?"

The cops circled behind Craig as he leaned on the Land Rover. He kept wishing that Gates would do something, glancing over at the ghost and willing him to act. But Gates retreated, his expression still blank, until he was almost invisible.

"God damn," Craig murmured as Halloran frisked him.

"Now what might this be?"

The chief took the BB gun and the walkie-talkie from Craig's jacket.

"Not looking good for you, son," the cop said. "Two weapons, wandering around the woods at night. And a shortwave radio? Not something your ordinary tourist would have. And then there's the situation at the hotel—all that noise and shouting, that poor old gentleman so shocked that he ended up needing hospital treatment. I guess we'll have to lock you up until we can get this confusing situation sorted out."

"Look, I can—hey!" Craig protested as Halloran grabbed his arms and held his wrists behind his back.

"Cuff him, Chet," the chief said.

Craig felt the cold metal of handcuffs snap tightly on his wrists.

"Gates!" Craig shouted plaintively.

But there was no sign of the ghost.

Halloran dragged him upright and then leaned close to whisper in Craig's ear.

"Gates can't help you, son. He may well have damned you."

"What do you mean?" Craig asked.

There was no reply. Halloran shoved him toward the patrol car and deposited him in the back before getting in. The deputy drove back to town. As they reached the outskirts of Grendon Mill, the walkie crackled to life, and Craig heard Tara's voice.

"Craig? You there?"

Halloran picked the radio off the dash and looked at it for a moment.

"Craig?" Tara repeated more urgently. "We freed the hostage. We're bringing the kid to safety now. But the ghosts are a problem, Craig. Answer me. Are you okay?"

Halloran pushed the send button and whispered.

"Tara, I can't talk any louder…"

Craig lunged forward and yelled over the cop.

"It's Halloran, don't answer!"

The chief smiled at him.

"What's that?" Tara's voice sounded very weak and far away now.

"Best turn yourself in, young lady, or things will go badly for your boyfriend here," said Halloran in his normal voice, then switched off the walkie.

"You've got no sacrificial victim now," Craig said defiantly. "Tara will make sure the kid's safe, then report all this."

Halloran chuckled, and Craig felt even less sure of himself.

"And how," Halloran asked, "do you think your lady friend will go anywhere with four flat tires? Once we've got you safely locked up, we'll go back and deal with her."

Craig almost told them it wouldn't be as easy as the chief thought, but if they had no idea of how dangerous Tara could be, that was one surprise he didn't want to spoil.

There was no processing or questioning at the police station. Craig's belt and laces were taken, and he was uncuffed and shoved into a cell. His demands for a phone call were ignored, though Chet the stony-faced deputy seemed on the verge of smiling for the first time. Once the cops left, there was nobody else around. The silence was oppressive. The whole town was asleep, it seemed, except for the bad guys and their opponents. And, of course, the ghosts.

"Gates, why?" he whined, sitting down on the hard bed.

Then he decided he was being unfair. Gates was afraid of The Five and had no power to physically harm them, otherwise he'd have done so long ago. All he could do was delay and confuse his living enemies.

Presumably, then, Gates had gone to join Tara, who could in theory take out all of The Five.

Except that Gates couldn't communicate with Tara.

"Dammit. I'm an idiot."

Craig struggled to think straight. Now that the adrenaline rush was over, the lack of sleep hit him hard. Something didn't fit, something he should have spotted. Did The Five know about Tara's power? If not, she could probably beat both cops, maybe even kill them. But if The Five knew and had some means to counter psychokinesis…

The word sprang into his mind, and he blurted it out at the empty cell. "We."

Tara had said, "We freed the hostage," and yet, she had no one with her. Was she speaking of the team's collective effort? That sounded wrong.

Who else could be with her? Cappy, maybe? That seemed wildly improbable. The old man might not even be back in town after his ordeal at the laundromat. And who else was there to help?

The answer was surely there but seemed to dance out of Craig's grasp. He felt himself nodding, his eyelids heavy as lead. He snapped upright, then gave in to fatigue and lay down. The cell was not cold, but he covered himself with a thin blanket that smelled of sweat, beer, and urine. It seemed a trivial inconvenience given the circumstances, but it summed up Craig's situation. The Five were small-town villains, he thought, sitting in Grendon Mill for decades, in all that time failing to achieve anything but add to the world's death and misery.

And now those small-town villains had captured Craig Ellison.

CHAPTER 28

THE FIVE

Craig woke to a wall marked with graffiti, old and new. Random words and phrases challenged his brain. Then, he heard voices discussing something in matter-of-fact tones. It was almost reassuring until he remembered where he was.

He recognized Halloran's voice, though oddly muffled.

"I think it's worth a try. I could sense it. He had merged with Gates."

Another familiar voice, this time a woman's. The librarian, Hettie.

"That last time we used a seer, it didn't work."

"But we came close," Halloran said. "And we don't have time to debate."

"Thanks to you," the woman said. "You were overconfident. You let them escape."

Halloran began to reply, but a new voice cut him off. Again, it sounded familiar. The mellifluous tone was that of someone used to speaking to an audience. Paul Foster, the minister at the little church.

"There is no point in bickering. The discarnates said there was a third snooper who presumably had a vehicle. There might be trouble if we don't act swiftly, and we can't let this one go. Let us proceed with the incalling."

Craig rolled over and nearly fell off the narrow, hard bed. The Five were outside the cell. He had half expected the robes and masks from Gates' shared memories, but these were just ordinary townsfolk. Halloran and his deputy in their uniforms, the minister with his clerical collar, the librarian in a prim tweed two-piece suit. There was a fifth person, of course, someone Craig had not seen before. An older man of around seventy with iron-gray hair who was the only one looking into the cell.

"He's awake," the old guy said. "I daresay he's been listening."

"No matter," Hettie said. "Let's get going."

Chet opened the cell door, and both cops approached Craig as he scrambled off the bed. He decided to fight, to buy as much time as possible. He had an idea who Tara's newfound ally was, and it gave him hope. If he could delay the ritual long enough, help might come.

"Don't make this harder than it needs to be, son," Halloran said quietly.

Craig wondered if he could grab one of their guns, ruled it out at once, and backed up against the far wall of the cell. Halloran was holding the handcuffs as Chet closed in. Craig had not been in a fight since high school and had not been very scrappy then, but he had to try. He feinted a blow at the deputy's face with his right fist. Chet made to ward off the blow with both hands, and Craig got in a good left-handed gut punch. It was satisfying to hear the breath whoosh from the deputy's mouth. Craig brought up his knee as the man doubled over, but it only connected with the man's cheek, not his chin.

"Nice try."

Craig heard Halloran's remark as the man's fist connected with his face. He stumbled and tried to regain his balance. Before he could, Chet had recovered and returned the gut punch with interest. After that, Craig lost track of the blows until he was hauled upright. He ached from a dozen bruises and blood streamed from his nose.

"That was just the kind of time-wasting we were talking about," Hettie remarked sourly. "And you've shed his blood prematurely."

Halloran swore as he fastened the cuffs too tightly on Craig's wrists.

"It won't matter, if we're right about the link to Gates," the chief said. "Now let's get going."

It was just after dawn, and there was nobody about as Craig was half-dragged, half-carried to an unmarked SUV. He licked drying blood from under his nose and yelled for help. Chet, still expressionless, shoved something into his mouth that smelled of sweat and cheap body spray. They manhandled Craig into the vehicle and pushed him onto the floor.

This was the moment when, in other circumstances, Craig might have called upon a ghost to do something. Anything. A ghost could reach inside a living man and crush his heart or scramble his brain if you could persuade them to do it. Craig, ever compassionate, ever persuasive, had done it.

It had begun by chance, an individual discovered by Chloe to be depraved, cruel, and an abuser of his family. Billy had killed the man without Craig saying a word. He'd been shocked at first, but Stark had convinced him to see it differently. There was a kind of wild justice in the killing. Other people deserved to die even more than the abuser.

Or so Stark insisted. Each time, one of the ghosts had confirmed that, yes, the individual Stark targeted was indeed a gangster, a torturer, or a corrupter of innocence. And Craig, because the money was good, had shoved down and out of sight all thoughts of morality. Of whether he had the right to judge and execute others, even if it was by phantom proxy.

Am I any better than these people? he thought. *They are after power and glory and all the usual crap. And I got a paycheck that actually let me live an okay existence.*

Then he thought of the discarnates. Of Chloe's friend, Nikki. Of the girl holding the grumpy cat. Of all the lost and confused and frightened people in the world, especially the young struggling on the verge of adulthood.

No. He was not as bad as The Five, nowhere near.

Craig was angry with himself, at his weakness and stupidity. He'd stumbled around like an idiot from the start of this half-baked quest. He'd been out of his depth from the moment he'd met the fake Tara and not even thought to verify her identity. And now, he faced the ultimate abyss. The incalling.

Memories of the dozen or more incallings Gates had endured flooded Craig's mind. Monstrous, hideous torture, gradually refined over the years, suffered by the innocent. All to torment the soul of an unlikely hero.

Something else became clear, something he had not grasped before. The Five wanted Gates to reveal the location of the amulet. But if that was impossible, they probably wanted him gone. To move on. To destroy him in such a way that he would no longer haunt the woods, and no longer be connected to the amulet. Leaving the precious object unguarded, unshielded from The Five's powers.

Craig felt further shame at his unheroic efforts, but it soon turned to rage. He was damned if he would just give in. There must be something he could do to thwart The Five and end their reign of terror. He suddenly realized that if he could kill them all today, he would. If he died in the process, it would be a worthwhile sacrifice.

The car slowed to a halt, and Craig ran through his options. They would have to jostle him out. He doubted they would free his hands, and he would not achieve much by kicking. But he was a decent runner, and if he had a chance, he could flee into the woods, the part opposite the haunted area.

"Here you go," Halloran said.

Craig sensed movement above him. Then something cold jabbed into the back of his neck, and a jolt of energy shot through his body. When the effects of the Taser had worn off, he was already being carried into the woods on some kind of stretcher. His hands were now fastened in front with zip ties. Judging by the growing pain in his ankles, they were bound, too.

His slim chance of escape was gone.

CHAPTER 29
THE INCALLING

The discarnates slowly revealed themselves.

At first, Craig heard distant shrieks and moans, chilling but pitiful. Then, twisting his head to look sideways into the trees, he saw what might have been the shadows of saplings move and twist to become the distorted limbs of the ghosts. Pale ovals became simplified, contorted faces, often almost invisible when the morning sun cast bright beams onto the forest floor.

"They're more restless than usual," Hettie said. "This is not the right time."

"We have no goddamn choice," Halloran grated. "I don't know how that little bitch got away from them, but we can't wait around to find out if she has any other tricks up her sleeve."

The ghosts drew closer, and Craig wondered if they might attack. These were not normal circumstances. It might be worth a try. He shook his head, heaved, worked his tongue, and the improvised gag fell from his mouth. It was, Craig saw with mild curiosity, a black glove, now covered with saliva.

"Kill them!" he shouted. "Kill them! Kill them all!"

Cursing, Chet grabbed the glove and forced it back into Craig's mouth. Hettie leaned over and grabbed Craig's head to hold him steady. As Chet gagged him again, Craig heard Halloran start to chant something in a language he didn't recognize. The others joined in, a little raggedly at first, but it gained volume and clarity. The discarnates continued to circle the party but didn't come near.

Halloran then gestured, and The Five stopped chanting.

"There are too many of them," hissed the unknown member of The Five. "We made a rod for our own backs here."

"We can't back out now," Halloran snapped. "Stay focused. I can feel Gates watching us. He's nearby."

Craig, too, could sense the dead psychic's presence. He could also hear Gates' voice, but the words were too faint. He wondered where Tara was, and if he was right in his guess about how she'd freed the captive. If he was wrong… Well, it was pointless to speculate. All he could do was be ready to do something—anything—to win this one.

They reached a familiar clearing, pleasant in the sunlight. The air had lost all trace of nighttime chilliness. It might have been an idyllic scene if there had been birdsong instead of the cries of distorted ghosts. The discarnates still circled, but now, they had started to talk about the suffering to come. Each one seemed to have its own deranged monologue, delivered without regard to what the others said. Some spoke of the horrors inflicted on their own bodies. A few giggled, some sobbed. Craig glimpsed Nikki, small with a blur of blue above her heart-shaped face.

The Five deposited Craig on the slab and tied him down. Then, they quickly put on their robes and masks, resuming their incomprehensible chant as they did so. Some of the discarnates darted forward, lingering nearby for a few seconds as if playing a game. One especially long-limbed entity struck out at Hettie in her cat mask and she gave a little shriek, interrupting the chant.

"Stay focused," Halloran urged. "All of one mind."

Craig tried to spit out the improvised gag again, but it was too tightly wedged. As The Five's chant became louder and more complex, he felt an odd numbness start to spread through his body. This, he felt sure, was the precursor to his soul being expelled, or partly so. Even Gates had not been clear on the details of the incalling, as he had only experienced it as massive trauma.

In desperation, Craig called out with his mind. He had the vague idea that Gates, a telepath, might hear him.

Help me, help me, help me.

Kill them, kill them, kill them.

Craig's internal mantra clashed with the chanting of The Five. He listened for some change in the crazy outpourings of the discarnates. Some faltered, and his hopes rose. But then, he felt a hideous wrenching sensation, and without warning, he was looking down at his own body on the slab. He looked pathetically small and weak. A glowing thread, just barely visible, reached from Craig's insubstantial form to link him to his mortal being.

Expressionless masks turned up to face him. Gates appeared, foreshortened from Craig's perspective, materializing slowly at the edge of the clearing. The Five's chant changed again, and Craig expected to feel the last frail link to his corporeal form severed. Instead, something even stranger happened. Gates drifted over to the slab and faded, his insubstantial form merging with Craig's inert flesh.

"Now we have them both."

Halloran's triumphant cry seemed to echo across the universe as a great darkness embraced Craig. Then he was looking up again, out of his own eyes. But he was also Gates, the veteran, the psychic, the Vegas performer, and the improbable hero. This time, he was not swamped with Gates' intense personality. Instead, he was almost fused with it. Almost, but not quite. There was still some semblance of individuality, yet they shared their thoughts.

"Get ready, my friend."

Gates' words cut through The Five's chanting, which reached an almost frenzied pitch, and then stopped. Hettie, in her mask, leaned over with a pair of scissors and cut away Craig's shirt and pants. The old guy, masked as an owl, raised a vicious-looking dagger with a serrated blade. Spring sunlight flashed on the steel.

"Alva Gates, yield the amulet to us or suffer your final dissolution."

"What do they mean?" Craig asked Gates in his thoughts.

"They think I'll move on and leave this world because I'm linked to you now," Gates responded.

"Are they right?" Craig asked.

"The last time they had a seer—a weak one—they came close," Gates conceded. *"But that could have been a coincidence. They're desperate. Clutching at straws, I guess."*

This was no comfort to Craig. They were going to torture him to death. The knife descended, and slowly, the man in the owl mask made a shallow cut down Craig's abdomen. It stung, but not too badly. From Gates' memories, Craig knew this could last for up to an hour, each cut worse than the last. If blood loss was minimal, his agony would be prolonged.

The leader of The Five began to cut across the first wound. A cross. A parody of faith, perhaps. The librarian leaned forward, producing a small jar from her robe that contained a white powder. She delicately sprinkled some into the wound. It stung ferociously. Craig screamed, but it was muffled. He heard a chuckle, probably from Chet.

"Salt," Gates explained needlessly. *"Normally they'd wait a lot longer, they must be rattled. You ready?"*

"For what?"

Craig sensed Gates' surprise at his puzzlement.

"Ready to rumble, of course. We're not going down without a fight, my friend."

CHAPTER 30
FOUR AGAINST FIVE

Owl Face made another cut, this one diagonally across Craig's chest, just above the heart. More salt followed. Tears streamed down Craig's face as he writhed.

"Make it easy on yourself—yourselves," the leader said. "This can end swiftly, or it can take what will seem like an eternity."

The old man took a few steps to the side, moving down Craig's body. The knife was now poised above his groin, the bloodied point aimed downward. Craig heard another chuckle.

"If you're going to do something, please do it now," he said to Gates.

The blade descended and then stopped, hovering just a few inches from Craig's flesh. Seconds passed. What seemed like gloating cruelty started to seem strange. Then, the arm holding the knife started to rise before bending at the elbow until the bloodstained point was aimed right at the throat of the leader.

"What…" croaked the voice from the mask. "What's happening? Somebody…"

The knife quivered, the fingers clutching it relaxing as it fell, but only for a moment. Then the blade twirled through the air, spun around in an arc, and descended toward the slab. Craig flinched, but the knife didn't strike him. Instead, it sliced through the ropes that secured his right arm.

"Stop it!" Halloran roared, lunging for the knife.

The blade slashed at his fingers, and he backed away. After the initial shock, the others were moving now. Chet tore off his wolf mask and reached inside his robe. The knife set Craig's other arm free and then clattered down beside him onto the bloodstained stone. Tara appeared at the edge of the clearing at the same time. She held an iron dagger in one hand and a Taser in the other.

Two discarnates closed in behind her. Craig shouted a warning, but it was needless.

The man he had met at the pub, Shane Ryan, appeared from the shadows and took a swing at the nearest phantom. It reeled back with a yelp, emitting a great cloud of dark particles. The man, his face impassive, struck again, and the ghost yelped before escaping into the trees.

"This is it, my friend. Move."

Craig didn't need prompting. He grabbed the knife and hacked at the ropes that bound his feet.

The Five had unmasked themselves now, except for the leader. In a matter of moments, they had gone from arrogant dominance to full fight-or-flight mode. The minister was already backing away from Tara and Shane. The librarian seemed unable to think of what to do, her eyes darting between the newcomers and Craig. Chet drew his gun, but before he could aim, a dagger flew from Tara's grasp at a terrifying speed and embedded itself in his right forearm. The deputy fell to his knees, howling and clutching at the wound.

Halloran aimed at Shane from about six feet away. The strange man saw the gun being leveled and sprang toward the police chief, going into a forward roll. Halloran fired, but his shot went way too high. Shane took the man's legs out from under him, and Halloran's gun went flying.

A discarnate lashed out, seemingly at random, its fingers grazing Halloran's back. Craig instinctively stabbed the shadowy arm and the ghost retreated, screeching.

Chet pulled Tara's dagger from his arm and lunged at Shane left-handed. Craig kicked out and deflected the blow. Chet turned on Craig, his face no longer expressionless. The deputy was raging and eager to kill, but he was very shaky, and it wasn't hard to see why. The man's right arm hung limply, his sleeve dark with blood.

"Don't do it!" Craig yelled.

The deputy gave a smile that was half snarl and came on. Craig backed into the slab and kicked out again but missed the hand holding the knife. Chet started to weave the dagger back and forth, smirking, enjoying Craig's terror.

"You can do it, buddy."

Gates' thought coincided with a sudden cool determination in Craig. He anticipated Chet's thrust and easily parried with his own blade. Then he jabbed toward the deputy's face, only aiming to put the man off-balance and drive him back. Chet lost his footing at the same moment, though, and the dagger entered his right eye. Craig felt the blade slide into soft tissue and grate against bone.

"Oh God," he gasped, feeling as if he was about to puke.

Chet fell backward, the knife hilt protruding from his eye socket as he crashed to the forest floor and lay still. Craig stood for a moment, looking at the body. Then he saw Shane pulling Halloran's robe back from his shoulders to immobilize him. Tara had grabbed Hettie and was holding her like a human shield, her Taser poised by the woman's neck. Two remaining discarnates hovered a few yards away, confused as to who, if anyone, they could attack. The leader and the minister were nowhere to be seen.

"This is murder," Halloran shouted, lying face down in the weeds. "You'll never get away with this. You bastards just killed a cop."

"You gonna call the FBI, maybe have them wander around these woods for a few days?" Shane countered, standing over the cop. "Hell no. You're not going to tell anyone about this. Also, if you get the time, maybe look up 'irony' in the dictionary."

Tara shoved Hettie face-down onto the slab and used the ropes to tie her up.

Shane walked up to Craig.

"I know it's hard, fella, but it was you or him," Shane said, picking up a discarded robe and handing it to Craig. "The question now is what happens next?"

Shane meant how they should handle the surviving members of The Five, but as Craig wrapped himself in the dark red robe, a different answer popped into his head. It wasn't hard to guess who was prompting him.

"We find the amulet," Craig said. "That will help solve the problem. I'm sure of it."

Shane looked puzzled for a moment, then shrugged.

"Okay. Where is this… amulet?"

Craig told him. The location was burned into his memory because it was still linked to Gates' memory. They left Halloran and Hettie protesting and cursing and set off in a northwest direction toward the densest part of the forest. Two and then three discarnates followed, keeping well out of range of the whirling blades and Shane's fists. Craig took point, with Shane covering the rear. Tara, who had barely spoken since she'd rescued Craig, walked slowly, and stumbled a few times. Eventually, Shane walked alongside her, helping her stay upright.

"This psychic thing takes it out of you, huh?"

"You could say that," she replied with a wan smile. "Energy… can't be created or destroyed… just transformed."

Shane mulled that over for a second, then looked at Craig.

"And what are we going to transform this Gates guy into? That's part of the plan, right?"

Craig felt another answer emerge, clear and sharp, in his head.

"Transcendence," he said. "From a ghost to something else. Something better."

"Gotcha," Shane said. "Private First Class Gates finally gets his service medal. About damn time."

CHAPTER 31
TRANSCENDENCE

The tree was a vast ancient oak, its gnarled trunk about four feet across. Craig wondered how it had escaped the lumberjacks when Grendon Mill was built. Perhaps it was too majestic and imposing.

Even the most cynical businessman might spare such a tree, Craig thought.

"Nah. It's just that the woods are dense here, so it's awkward to get at."

Gates was not quite taking over Craig as he had been back at the hotel, but there was still a connection. It was like the effect of a powerful dream that still possessed the dreamer after waking. Only in this case, the dream was not fading. Not yet at least.

"We didn't bring shovels," Shane observed sourly. "How deep is this guy buried?"

"Not buried at all," Craig assured him. "He just crawled into a cavity. I guess he'll be well-covered with leaf mold by now."

Craig and Shane improvised crude tools from fallen branches and cleared out the space where Gates, mortally wounded, had hidden so many years ago. They soon found remains that nature had long since claimed. Most of Gates' bones were in situ, but there were signs of predation. Skin, muscle, and internal organs were long gone. Gates' clothes had fared much better. The effect was weird—browned and gnawed remains partially wrapped in gaudy synthetic fiber.

"Guess bugs don't eat nylon," Craig murmured.

"Surprising how little time it takes for a body to get recycled," Tara said. "Foxes, beetles, flies, whatever. They take it all back."

"Apart from the soul," Craig added quietly.

He knelt and crawled into the cavity. Gates' skull grinned at him in the half-light, a startled spider mimicking a rolling eyeball in one empty socket. Craig remembered the Vegas showman preening himself in the dressing room mirror. A familiar voice spoke in his head.

"No need to rub it in."

Craig had to smile even as he reached out to shift Gates' ribcage.

Gates had died with his right arm bent under him. Craig exposed the clenched fist and gently forced apart the fingers. Something gleamed. He touched cold metal. He heard Shane asking a question nearby but could not make out the words. Gates was speaking again.

"Sorry about this, Craig. It's gonna hurt, but I gotta use you as a launch pad."

"A what—?"

All of Gates' pain flooded through Craig. He went through the incallings and torture-murders again. He fought and was wounded in the burning mill. He struggled over the decades to keep the amulet hidden. He thwarted The Five as best he could, never moving on, never taking the easy way out. A kaleidoscope of emotions and memories exploded around him and through him. It was destroying him, and he knew the power of the amulet was making it possible.

"No, I don't... want... to die."

Gates' reply carried the veteran's grim humor.

"You'll be fine, just roll with it."

The pain was so intense that Craig could barely see what was happening around him. Yet, he was aware of a vast and overwhelming presence. Then, as suddenly as it had struck, the pain stopped. Craig lay in the dark hollow, still clutching the amulet, his perspective now almost godlike. Craig looked down on the scene, through the trees, and at his prone body. He saw Shane and Tara crouching nearby, and Shane reaching for Craig's ankles, but in slow motion.

And then, he looked up and saw a vortex of blue-white light, something like a galaxy but radiating heat that flowed through him. It swirled above him, a gap in the fabric of reality, a whirlpool drawing Gates into some other dimension. It was drawing energy from Craig in some way.

"Focus on it, Craig," Gates urged. *"Hold the doorway open. You can do it."*

Craig did his best, concentrating on the idea of an open door, a threshold that could be crossed. He glimpsed the ghost one last time. Gates was smiling as he finally left this world, still clad in his lurid outfit, complete with chest medallion. It made an interesting contrast to the dazzling whiteness of the vortex above them.

"Leaving you a gift for services rendered. And beware of…"

The voice faded before Gates finished his warning. The spirit was gone. The whirlpool of radiance shrank, its color changing from blue to yellow to smoky red. Then, Craig was being hauled out from among the tree roots.

"I'm okay," he managed to croak. "Just… he's gone. He moved on."

"Did you get it?" Tara asked.

He opened his fist. In it lay a diamond-shaped piece of metal that might have been silver. It showed no sign of tarnish.

"Doesn't look like much," Shane remarked, helping Craig to sit up. "What you gonna do with it?"

Craig looked at Tara.

"I guess we finish the job we were contracted to do," she said wearily. "Unless you've got a better idea?"

Before Craig could think about it, the three discarnates that had tracked them reappeared. Shane saw them at once, and Tara was quick to read the situation. She stood and took out a dagger as Shane moved to stand alongside her. However, the spindly entities did not attack. Instead, they wafted back and forth, staying out of reach, and making fretful noises.

Then, the smallest of the three spoke. Craig recognized Chloe's long-lost friend, Nikki, from the slight blue aura around the mournful face.

"Is it true? Can we be free?"

Craig remembered what Gates had said about using him as a launch pad. He looked down at the amulet. It had the power of transcendence, to move a spirit that might otherwise tarry forever on Earth. Could Craig do that for other ghosts? What else might Gates have meant when he said he was leaving Craig a gift?

He stepped forward, holding up the amulet.

"I think I can help you move on, Nikki."

"Careful," Shane warned as Craig kept walking past his companions, holding out both hands in welcome and supplication. Nikki hesitated, darting back, and then stopping. The other two discarnates moved off but did not vanish, stopping a dozen yards away. The sense of expectation was palpable.

"You sure you can do it?" Tara asked.

"I've got to try," Craig said.

He halted just out of reach, giving Nikki the option to approach. The ghost quivered, emitting a moan that suggested equal parts fear and indecision. Then, a weirdly contorted arm reached out, and small fingers brushed against Craig's hand. The amulet gave out a pulse of energy like a mild electric shock. And suddenly, Craig could feel Nikki's fear, loneliness, and despair. It was an imperfect melding, nothing as intense as it had been with Gates. But amid the jumble of memories, he found Chloe, Nikki's family, and the trials of adolescence. Then came the journey into the woods, the capture, and the incalling.

Craig focused on what had happened to Gates. He looked up and recreated the feeling of blazing light and comforting warmth. He cleared his mind of extraneous thoughts until there was nothing in the universe but him and Nikki. Transcendence was attainable.

"Believe, Nikki. Believe it is possible," Craig spoke to Nikki in his mind.

The vortex appeared again, bright but not as dazzling as before. Craig again visualized the threshold, the portal to a better existence. He willed it to stay open and urged Nikki's spirit to rise and be free. He sensed her exhilaration, and the sudden outpouring of hope as she started to rise.

Then she, too, was gone.

CHAPTER 32
AFTERMATH

"What happened?"

Shane was speaking, standing right next to him. Craig looked around in confusion and saw Tara's puzzlement.

What had happened? He felt light-headed, unable to organize his thoughts.

"Did it work?" Tara demanded.

"I think…"

Craig was about to say that it seemed to have worked, but he saw a small, hunched form half-hidden in the shadows nearby. It was Nikki, or rather, her tormented spirit. Craig heard sobbing, and his heart sank. He had failed. Whatever part he had played in Gates' transcendence, he had achieved nothing with Nikki. By extension, he could not help any of the discarnates.

"It didn't work," he said flatly.

"Figures," Tara said. "They didn't die natural deaths. They're not regular ghosts like Gates was. Maybe they can never move on."

"I don't want to believe that," Craig snapped. "There must be some way to help them."

Shane said nothing but peered through the trees at the other two discarnates. Craig saw those ghosts move slowly toward Nikki as if to check on her. Then he heard their distorted, eerie voices.

"The Five, The Five, took our lives and afterlives."

"Cursed forever, here forever."

"Evil, evil!"

"Hopeless, hopeless!"

The two spirits began to move faster, heading toward the group by the oak.

"Get ready, they're coming," Shane warned Tara.

"I don't think it's us they want," Craig said quietly. "Just step aside."

Shane looked skeptical but did as Craig suggested. The two phantoms passed, blurred faces turned briefly toward the living. Then they moved on into the trees and were lost to sight.

"What happened? Did they just go?" Tara asked.

Craig offered an explanation.

"The Five had power over them, but now that there are only four, I suspect whatever clout they wielded is gone, or so weak that—"

"Their victims are out for revenge," Shane cut in. "Figures."

As if to confirm it, a piercing howl rang through the woods. It was followed by a voice that Craig recognized as Halloran's. He couldn't make out the words, but it wasn't hard to recognize pleading in the tone. Then came more cries of pain and fear, followed by an ominous silence.

"What if they just start randomly attacking people?" Tara asked. "They're crazy enough, and we know they can reach the town."

Craig went over to Nikki, who was now standing forlornly nearby, still sobbing.

"Will you kill innocent people, Nikki? Is that what you want?"

"No," she said. *"They made us do bad things. We were never bad, we were just hurt. Lost."*

Craig relayed that to Tara. Shane grunted but did not comment. Craig turned back to Nikki, who was drifting away forlornly.

"I promise I'll come back and help you."

The ghost shrank to a blurred mound of shadow.

"Promises. Promises are so simple. But hard to see through."

"I will come back," Craig said quietly.

There was no response. After a few moments, it was impossible to say if Nikki was still there amid the dappled patches of sunlight.

"It's nasty, I know," Tara said, "but at least there won't be any survivors to found a new cult of Five."

They made their way back to the road, where Shane's beat-up sedan was parked by Tara's Discovery. There was a brief, almost surreal discussion of whether Shane's car could tow Tara's to the nearest garage. They decided not to risk it, opting instead to call a tow truck when she got a signal.

It was all so normal, like nothing out of this world had just happened, which made it doubly bizarre. Shane shrugged as Craig explained this.

"You get used to it. Life goes on."

Tara took a small first aid kit from her car and Shane drove them back into Grendon Mill. They saw flashing lights as they approached the hotel, a crowd, and a small traffic jam. They slowed. A body, covered from head to foot, was being lifted into the back of an ambulance. Shane rolled down the window and beckoned one of the gawkers.

"What happened?"

"Seems like the minister got killed in a hit-and-run," the man replied. "They just found him there, lying in the road."

Shane thanked the bystander and they drove slowly past the little tableau and parked.

"You think they got all five by now?" Craig asked.

"We'll soon find out," Tara said. "All prominent local citizens. All except for the leader. Who was that guy?"

Craig sifted through what remained of Gates' memories. Many had already slipped away or become vague.

"I've no idea," he said. "Guess it wasn't important."

After they parked, Tara used the first aid kit to clean and dress Craig's wounds. They were not too deep, but he would have to see a doctor soon, she declared, before going to his room to get him yet another change of clothes. Craig, hunched down in the back of the sedan to avoid prying eyes, thanked Shane profusely for his help. The other man shrugged it off.

"No biggie."

"How did you link up with Tara in the first place?"

"She sent me some drone pics, and I figured out a way to sneak up and reconnoiter."

Craig fell silent, pondering his brush with death. Now that the rush of excitement had died down, he felt inadequate. He had been fooled too often and never been properly prepared. Without the help of Gates and then Shane, he'd have been dead and maybe gotten Tara killed, too.

Shane twisted around in the driver's seat.

"Tara said this was your first real taste of front-line action?"

"You could call it that," Craig said, staring down at the amulet. "I wasn't ready. Maybe I'll never be."

"Fate rarely calls upon us at a moment of our choosing," Shane said.

Craig looked up. It sounded like a quotation, which seemed surprising coming from a man like Shane. Then he felt slightly ashamed for assuming the guy didn't read books.

"Was that Napoleon?" Craig asked. "Or one of those ancient Greek guys?"

"Optimus Prime."

CHAPTER 33

MOVING ON

After Craig got back to his hotel room, he showered and then collapsed on his bed. He slept from just before eight to nearly midday. There was a strange woman in his room when he woke.

"Hello?" he said, sitting up.

The woman's eyes widened. Craig, rubbing his eyes, noticed she was dressed a little oddly in an old-fashioned maid's outfit: black dress and stockings, shiny black shoes, a white hat, and an apron. She looked about forty, but it was hard to tell. She had a careworn, miserable look.

"I can see you," Craig added quietly. "It's okay."

The maid started to whimper, rubbing her nose, which was red at the tip.

"Can you help me?" she asked. "I've been here so long. I didn't do anything wrong, and I'm so lonely, and they said you could help me, so I thought…"

Craig sat up, suddenly aware that he was almost naked. The maid stopped talking and stared at the dressings on his chest and torso.

"Oh, they hurt you. You poor thing."

Craig's heart went out to the ghost.

"Who told you I could help?"

"It was a girl. One of the strange ones. We don't usually talk to them. They're too… wild. But now that The Five are gone, it's easier for us to communicate with the strange ones because we don't have to hide from The Five anymore."

"Why did you hide from The Five?" Craig asked.

"They wanted to use us," she said. "To enslave us like the strange ones. Make us find something for them. So we hid."

"That must have been kind of boring," Craig said.

The maid gave a little shrug. Lurking out of sight for a few decades didn't matter much to a being condemned to walk the earth forever, but it clearly hadn't improved her morale.

"Will you help me?" she asked. "Please. If you can. The girl said you're a good man."

Craig remembered Nikki vanishing in the woods. She must have ventured into town, at least as far as the maid's haunting ground. The word would, no doubt, spread. Perhaps other ghosts would want to move on. He might be stuck here for days.

No, he rebuked himself. *Not stuck. Being useful.*

"I'll try," he said and held out his hands.

The maid, hesitant at first, took a couple of steps and reached out. Craig saw her hands were small, the fingernails cut close to the quick. A working woman's hands. There was nothing on the ring finger. He wondered how lonely she had been in life, working at this hotel, and perhaps dreaming of a better life, of romance, and excitement.

He wondered who or what had killed her, and why her death had led to her lingering here. But that didn't matter. This was not a talking cure. He had to see if he could succeed where he had failed with Nikki.

Their fingertips merged and he felt a tingle midway between a shock and a chill. It was a gentle collision of souls, nothing like interacting with Gates or the discarnates. Instead, the maid's life appeared as a kind of four-dimensional movie, a small and sad array of memories blossoming in Craig's mind. Her name was Anita. She had loved someone, but the Spanish Flu had claimed him in 1918, and she had nursed her grief until a greater tragedy struck. She had been shy and easily swayed, and a long-dead hotel manager had taken advantage of that. Lies, abuse, and finally murder. Anita's bones lay under the concrete floor of the old laundry room. She had been twenty-seven when she died, not forty. The poor aged faster in those days.

All this passed in an instant. Craig set aside the sadness and focused on helping her move on.

It proved easier than he had thought. Summoning the memory of Gates' transcendence, focusing on that shining vortex high above, brought it into being. It was, Craig supposed, like saying a magic word. But whatever the reason, the ghost was suddenly transformed. Now her face glowed with a golden light, and her eyes shone with happiness as she looked up at the portal to somewhere unimaginable to living humans.

It was over almost before it had begun. Craig was sitting on the edge of the bed, hands outstretched, looking at a damaged hotel sofa. He felt a wave of exhaustion flow through him and slumped sideways, sighing. No pain, but Tara had been right about energy. It had to come from somewhere, and it seemed that he was the source. Gates had gifted him with a neat power, but he would have to use it sparingly.

The cuts he had sustained throbbed a little more noticeably now. He'd taken some strong painkillers, but they were wearing off. He had to see a doctor, and the nearest ER was miles away. A tetanus shot would be a good idea. Then there was the question of lunch. They could hit Dinah's Diner again. He sat up and reached for his phone, then stopped to stare.

The amulet was lying next to his phone.

I didn't need it.

Craig had assumed the power Gates conferred on him worked through the amulet or was boosted by it, but that wasn't so. Whatever the thing did, it wasn't necessary to help the dead move on. He picked up the diamond-shaped sliver of metal and examined it closely. There was a suggestion of engraving on one side, but years of handling had almost worn away the pattern. Was it a beast of some kind, like a heraldic dragon? He wasn't sure.

He stood, shoved the amulet into the back pocket of his jeans, and called Tara.

Twenty minutes later, they were back in the town square, heading for the diner, and discussing their next move. Tara said Shane had already gone after asking some questions about Stark and other matters.

"I get the impression," she said, "that he wants us to keep him informed. He thinks there's something damn sketchy about this quest. He's right, of course."

Craig was about to reply when he spotted Cappy sitting on his usual bench facing the town hall. The old man was talking to a big, bearded man in a flannel shirt, jeans, and heavy work boots. Craig had never seen anyone who looked so much like a lumberjack.

"You see that guy with the beard talking to Cappy?" he asked Tara, pointing.

She looked and shook her head.

"Thought so. Gimme a minute."

Cappy and the big man watched him approach. Up close, the latter was clearly from a bygone era. When he grinned at Craig, his teeth were like a smashed piano keyboard, and there were no logos on anything he wore.

"Here he is," Cappy said. "Ghostbuster supreme."

"Glad to see you…" Craig hesitated. He could hardly say "looking well", as Cappy didn't. He opted to finish the greeting with, "out and about."

Cappy grunted, or maybe it was a laugh.

"Guess I'm lucky. Guess the whole town's lucky. Things might be a bit better around here from now on."

Craig waited for thanks, but they didn't come. So he spoke to the ghost instead.

"I suppose you know I can help people move on?" he asked.

The big man's grin faded. Then he faded, his body swiftly becoming transparent until Craig and Cappy were alone.

"Some folks don't want to move on," the old man said. "Important life lesson there. Or death lesson. Take your pick."

They stayed in town for another day while Tara's car got fixed. Craig encountered a couple more ghosts who wanted to move on and helped them. When they drove out of Grendon Mill early the following morning, they encountered a small convoy of vehicles heading into town.

"State troopers," Tara remarked. "Somebody noticed that the police chief and his deputy vanished without a trace."

Craig wondered how the outsiders would handle the search. He would check for news updates, rumors, and conspiracy theories about Grendon Mill for weeks. And he would go back. No matter how long it took, no matter what he had to endure, he would help the discarnates. He was as sure of that as he was ignorant of how to help.

Once they were on the highway, he let sleep claim him. When he woke, they were already in familiar suburbs, passing a Waffle House he'd been to a few times. Hours had passed. The town's bars would be open.

"You ready for this?" Tara said. "We could always hold off for a few hours."

"Nah, I'm good."

Tara had parked a couple of blocks from Hannigan's. They had put the amulet into a small case with a combination lock. Tara carried it and Craig looked around nervously while trying to seem nonchalant. It would be the ultimate irony for a random mugger to snatch the thing so many had suffered and died for. But they got to the pub unscathed.

Around Hannigan's, Craig saw the usual gathering of spirits yearning to enter but eternally barred. It suddenly occurred to him that the amulet, being a magical item, might also be excluded by whatever power protected

Hannigan's. He mentioned this to Tara.

"I guess that depends," she said, hesitating on the corner. "People with psychic powers—like you—aren't excluded. Artifacts aren't beings. Anyway, we'll find out soon."

Craig stepped inside and held the door for Tara. She held the case in front of her, took a step forward, and frowned. Then she took another step and was across the threshold, on the faded carpet.

"Slight resistance," she said quietly. "But just for a second. Whatever, Stark told us to come here, and we came."

There were only a handful of customers. Melody flashed Craig a smile from behind the counter. Harry was at one end of the bar deep in conversation with Cal, the antique dealer. Stark sat at the opposite end. The middleman was unusually well-dressed in an electric blue suit. The effect was undermined by scuffed tennis shoes.

"Ah, the wanderers return," he boomed as Tara and Craig sat down. "And after quite an ordeal. Mr. Ryan not with you?"

Tara and Craig had spoken to Stark the previous evening, giving just the bare facts, and omitting any mention of Craig's newfound ability. They had, however, emphasized the role Shane Ryan had played.

"No," Tara said, "he had other business to attend to."

"A most competent man," Stark mused, looking at the case Tara had placed on the bar. "And not asking for remuneration? That makes him doubly interesting. In my experience, a man who can't be bought is a rarity. But perhaps there's more to his situation than meets the eye…"

He paused. Melody dawdled a few yards away. Craig ordered a lite beer and Tara joined him. After they'd been served and Melody had gone to join Harry and Cal, Stark opened the case.

"Remarkable," he said in awe. "And you say it had the power to help this Gates person ascend to a higher plane?"

"Yes, I saw it happen," Craig said.

Stark picked up the amulet and turned it over with slightly stubby fingers. He frowned at the worn pattern and then set the amulet on the bar. He scrabbled around in his pocket and, to Craig's surprise, took out a green crayon. Then he picked up a napkin from a holder and laid it on the amulet. Rubbing the napkin with the crayon revealed details that were hidden from the naked eye.

The worn engraving was that of an uncoiling serpent which seemed to have six tentacles emerging from behind its head. But before Craig could examine the image more closely, Stark crumpled the napkin and shoved it into one of his bulging pockets.

"Great Cthulhu?" Tara suggested.

"Not exactly," Stark smiled, "but my client will be pleased. Now, as to your payment and expenses…"

As soon as he had paid them, Stark got off his barstool. This was unusual. Normally, he liked to hold court in Hannigan's, listening to gossip, offering to help innocent strangers, and being approached by shady characters whom he never named or introduced. But this particular afternoon, he seemed very eager to be gone. He had some parting words for them, though.

"The next little adventure might see you going overseas. Details are sketchy at the moment, but I assume you both have passports?"

Craig didn't, and Stark read his expression.

"Well, you'd better get busy on that paperwork, my friend. Get it expedited. My client has his eye on something rather special from the Old World. A rarity as strange and ancient as this amulet—but perhaps a little more dangerous. The financial incentive will increase accordingly, of course."

"Wonderful," Tara said. "I don't suppose you can tell us anything about this 'rarity' right now?"

Stark smiled and left without another word.

"What a smug piece of…" Tara's voice trailed off and she took a swig of her beer. "Reminds me of this professor."

She launched into a scurrilous anecdote as if she and Craig had been friends for years. Their laughter prompted Melody to drift over to them again.

"You guys look beat," said the barmaid while looking only at Craig. "Why do you work for that jerk?"

"M-O-N-E-Y," Tara said. "Times are hard."

"You got that right," Melody sighed. "You want another beer?"

Craig went home after depositing his check. His support group of ghosts was waiting, glad to see him, and impatient for an update.

He made himself some coffee and sat down, wondering how to begin. He knew what had happened to Chloe's friend and could not keep the truth from her. That was going to be a tough revelation. On the plus side, Craig now had a way to help them all move on if that was what they wanted.

"Okay guys," he said, putting his mug on the arm of the sofa. "I guess I've got some good news, and some bad news."

Epilogue

Peregrine Stark stepped into the vault and closed the heavy steel door behind him. The clang was muffled by heavy scarlet draperies and a dense carpet dyed a deep maroon. This was his special place, the inner sanctum where he kept his most prized possessions. Sensitive documents, precious stones, historic artifacts, and some very strange trophies were arranged on shelves or in glass-fronted cabinets.

He called it the Red Chamber.

As he walked across the room, Stark recalled the years he had spent amassing his collection. It was worth millions, perhaps tens of millions, in theory at least. If he was ever short of cash—which seemed absurdly improbable—he could sell some lesser item and be liquid again. But it was not the monetary value that mattered so much as the power and status his possessions conferred upon him. Such things were incalculable, but as real as any currency.

Of course, things had recently changed.

The Red Chamber was no longer a place of solitary pleasures.

Stark placed the case on the table at the center of the room and waited. Opposite the heavy vault door was another, much simpler and less imposing. It was covered in red leather and held in place with studs. The indirect lighting of the vault gave it a slightly oily, organic look that was, Stark felt, only appropriate.

"I have it."

There was no response.

"It is the amulet. Those who found it tasted its power, albeit briefly. I could not help that."

Again, silence filled the Red Chamber.

Then, almost imperceptibly, the red door began to open. There was no creak, not even a hint of well-oiled hinges in motion. Stark's breathing became fast and shallow. He looked down at the case on the table, not wanting to see but knowing he would have to. A wave of coldness swept over him, and he could not stop himself from shivering.

He had to look up.

When he did, he saw the Shadow. It was framed in a weak, bluish light that sometimes flickered and died then flared up again. The Shadow stepped into the vault, its blackness so intense that it was impossible to discern its outline. The cold increased as it approached the table, and then it stood, waiting. It was roughly the same height and build as the man facing it, yet Stark always felt it was bigger somehow.

Stark, his teeth chattering now, opened the case, and took out the amulet.

"See?" he said. "It is Yelbeghen, the seven-headed dragon. We have succeeded."

The Shadow waited, unmoving and silent, but Stark knew what it wanted. He always knew. Despite the piercing cold and the terror the thing inspired, he walked around the table and held out the precious find. In a moment, the amulet was around the Shadow's neck. The being shuddered and then grew, gaining three or four inches on Stark. He retreated to gaze at it, still shivering.

"Magnificent," he whispered, and his breath briefly clouded the air. "The first stage is complete."

Check out these best-selling series from our talented authors:

GHOST STORIES

RON RIPLEY
BERKLEY STREET SERIES
MOVING IN SERIES
HAUNTED COLLECTION SERIES
DEATH HUNTER SERIES

IAN FORTEY
JIGSAW OF SOULS SERIES
CULT OF THE ENDLESS NIGHT SERIES

SUPERNATURAL SUSPENSE

A. I. NASSER
SLAUGHTER SERIES
SIN SERIES

DAVID LONGHORN
NIGHTMARE SERIES
ASYLUM SERIES

SARA CLANCY
THE BELL WITCH SERIES
BANSHEE SERIES

For a complete list of our new releases and best-selling horror books, visit
ScareStreet.com or scan the QR code below!